EMERETT HAS NEVER BEEN IN LOVE

Love, Austen #1

ANYTA SUNDAY

First published in 2021 by Anyta Sunday
Buerogemeinschaft ATP24, Am Treptower Park 24, 12435 Berlin

An Anyta Sunday publication
www.anytasunday.com
Copyright 2021 Anyta Sunday

ISBN 978-3-947909-24-7

Cover Design & Illustrations by Lauren Dombrowski
www.laurendombrowski.com

Typography by Natasha Snow
www.natashasnow.com

Content Edit & Proofread by Lynda Lamb @ Refinery
www.refineryedits.com

Line Edited by HJS Editing
www.hjseditingservices.com

For Sunne, who makes me realize with every novel that I never know what day of the week it is.

Emerett Has Never Been In Love

A man who acts before he thinks, a man who thinks before he acts, and the ensuing mishaps on the path to the ultimate love match.

~ ~ ~

Emerett "Lake" Lakewood has a healthy ego and a flair for the dramatic. After losing his best friend to marriage—completely crushing his heart—he deems it prudent to distract himself, and what better way than playing cupid?

He's already got his eye on two young men desperately seeking romance, and he has a plan to hook them up.

Barbecues.

Photoshoots.

Reciting Shakespearean love declarations.

Lake is killing it. Love is positively *pulsing* in the air. Anyone could see it.

Well, anyone other than Knight, his best friend's dad, who cautions Lake to stop meddling. To leave love to its natural course.

Lake has always valued Knight's frankness, but this time he's wrong. Without him, two hearts might be doomed never to find love.

Besides, what does Knight know about romance? He's barely dated in all the seven years Lake's known him. He's clueless. Though, there's a thought. Knight has everything going for him. Sensibility. Kindness. Generosity. And for a forty-four-year-old, he's—objectively—freaking hot.

Why *is* he single?

~ ~ ~

". . . [T]here may be a hundred different ways of being in love."
~ Jane Austen

And a hundred different ways not to recognize it.

Cast

Emerett "Lake" Lakewood: Ridiculously clueless and a compulsive matchmaker.

Knightly Dixon: Morally scrupulous with the patience of a saint.

Taylor Dixon: Knightly's son and Lake's best friend.

Amy Dixon: Wife of Taylor, married off-page at the start of the book.

Harry: Lake's first victim of romantic meddling.

Philip: The man Lake wants Harry to fall in love with. Fond of clapping and his alligator-print shoes.

Martin: Harry's cousin and longstanding crush.

Cameron: Next door neighbor and huge fan of Jane Austen. Needs a venue for his film studio.

Brandon: Cameron's brother and business partner.

Josh: Lives down the street, graduated from Oxford, does everything better than Lake.

West: Lived abroad in England, was Taylor's first best friend. Is harboring a secret.

Garfield: The cat.

Emerett "Lake" Lakewood loved love, and *loathed* weddings.

He snatched the spare key from underneath a pot of petunias and broke into his best friend's childhood home. Floorboards creaked as he stole into the urban-farmhouse-style living room.

Taylor's Xbox shimmered in a shaft of moonlight; the distressed-wood coffee table he and Taylor had studied at for exams gleamed; the forest-green vase they'd taken turns throwing up in the night they'd graduated college taunted. A silly ache washed over him like a late October breeze.

He'd been one of the last to leave the local hall, though he'd wanted to bail the minute Taylor and Amy—his now wife —had driven off with a clatter of tin cans.

His sigh echoed in the room. From his tuxedo lapel, he removed a cream lily. The flower his best friend had chosen for the centerpieces and bouquet.

Lake set it atop the rustic mantelpiece, under an old clock that ticked ten past three, and slung himself lengthwise over the couch. He sank into its familiar hold, but it lacked comfort without Taylor trying to knock his legs away.

Lake buried a sad groan in a linen throw pillow.

He should be happy.

Taylor loved Amy, they were devoted to each other. Lake and Taylor had just turned twenty-six, for crying out loud. Dynamics changed with time. Best friends became friends, and then later, acquaintances. This was the natural course of life.

But, God. This sucked.

No best friend to listen to his crazy schemes and political tirades.

No best friend to give him advice on his boring commercial-editing job and his nonexistent love life.

No best friend to be blatantly open with.

He'd become a loner, suffering in bromantic solitude.

He punched the pillow over another self-pitying groan.

A darkened figure appeared in the doorway, brandishing Taylor's baseball bat. Lights flashed on, and Lake shielded his eyes. "Just add to the torture, why don't you."

"Lake?" Taylor's dad said, a surprised hitch in his low-timbred voice.

Lake lowered the pillow.

Taylor's dad—Knightly Dixon, or Knight, as Lake had been calling him daily for the last seven years—lowered the bat and threw his neatly tuxedoed ass into the adjacent armchair, gripping Taylor's bat like a king holding his staff. With his free hand, he loosened his bowtie and popped a button.

He looked nothing like Taylor. Taller, darker brown hair, squarer jaw, and deeper laughter creases. He'd shaved for the wedding, but he already sported light, silver-speckled stubble. A badge of raising a child alone in his twenties and thirties.

Okay sure, he had a good relationship—friendship?—with Taylor's dad. But Knight had a way of making Lake see his own faults. And Lake did not enjoy seeing his own faults . . .

Knight settled tired, soulful brown eyes on him. "What the hell are you doing here?"

Lake rolled onto his side, propped himself on his elbow, and stared at Knight's muddied dress shoes. "Did you walk back?"

"I'd hardly drive after drinking." He toed off his shoes and tossed them onto the tiled hearth.

"Guess I made you traipse in here with them on?"

"I saw a flicker in the window and grabbed this from the shed." Knight lifted the bat an inch off the ground and dropped it again. "I have a great deal of patience when it comes to you, Lake. But please, never scare me like that again."

"Mental note: Don't give Taylor's old man a heart-attack. Got it."

A pillow hit Lake smack-bang on his grin.

"Forty-four is not old."

"Says the forty-four year old."

Knight laughed. "You held yourself together today. Only spotted you bawling once."

"Behind the crostini station?"

"The men's room."

"Of course. The men's room. That was absolutely the only time." Lake sagged until his head hit the couch. "He's married. My Taylor. *Our* Taylor."

"You act like you'll never see him again. He's married and traveling Europe for a month, not transferring there for good. He lives three blocks from here."

"He'll miss us too, Knight. He might be shedding a few tears of his own right now."

"I certainly hope not."

"How are you okay with all this? He lived here until he was twenty-five."

"I'm okay with it because he lived here until he was twenty-five." Knight's blue gaze danced. "And he's okay with it because now he only has Amy's day to ask about, not both of ours."

"Especially since one response was always delightfully dramatic?" Lake teased. "Come on, I know that's what you're thinking."

"Exactly what I was thinking. And what I would have followed with."

Lake laughed and tucked the pillow Knight had thrown at him under his head. "You love telling me how it is, don't you?"

"It's kept me entertained for years."

Honesty triumphed because Knight knew flattery would inflate Lake's already robust ego.

Irritatingly wise man.

They stared vacantly into space. The air thickened, morosely, weighted with honeysuckle and a thousand memories they'd all shared in this room. It had so often been the three of them; everything felt off-balance now Lake and Knight were on their own. Like the Knight that Lake knew as Taylor's dad had to be relearned. Even though, factually, Lake knew everything about him already.

Confusing.

Knight rubbed the arm of his chair, staring toward him thoughtfully.

"Do you think he'll miss us?" Lake asked quietly.

"It'd be impossible not to miss one of us." Knight cleared his throat. "He'll also send more pictures than we'll know how to respond to. He and Amy will be smiling in all of them, and that will make me the happiest dad in the world."

Lake rolled toward Knight, absorbing his warm, solid smile. "Freeze. That beauty right there on your mug. Acknowledge I played a significant role in that. I hooked them up, after all."

Knight rolled his eyes, snorting. "Something you did with far too much glee, Lake. It's a surprise you bawled today at all."

"Matching them up, giving them advice, watching them fall in love . . . that was the fun part." He sighed. "I'll never forget the day they met. Pouring rain, Amy trudging her cat in a carrier and Taylor lugging your Garfield to the same vet. Me, the only one with an umbrella. Taylor admired pretty Amy and her plaited hair, and when it came time to leave, I took an extra-long time until Amy was done with the vet. Then I swapped Taylor my umbrella for the cat carrier and the rest, as they said today, is till death do us part." Lake grinned. "Maybe I need more of that."

"Garfield is due for her annual shots. Be my guest."

"It won't happen the same way twice. But bring on the falling in love."

Knight eyed him inquisitively. "For yourself this time?"

Lake barked out a laugh. "I'm never interested in the guys who are into me. Most are only into my looks." He waved a hand from his dark hair and model-like face to his perfectly proportioned body, blowing out a frustrated breath. "Love is supposed to be this amazingly powerful thing—and it happens all the time—but *I've* never felt it. Not with any of my exes. It's not for me."

Lake shoved a nervous hand through his hair, avoiding Knight's expression. No doubt he'd give logical advice on the situation, but Lake didn't want to hear it.

"So no," he continued, "not for me. But I did notice Philip watching Amy and Taylor like he wished it was his big day."

"Philip? The big-eared guy you and Taylor volunteer with at the food bank?"

"He also DJed, and his ears aren't that big. You know, you shouldn't identify people by their negative traits."

"What if I happen to like big ears on a man?"

"Do you?" Lake had hardly seen him date at all. But now that it was brought up . . .

Lake cocked his head. Objectively speaking, his best friend's dad was ridiculously handsome. Always had been. Why didn't he date more?

Knight rubbed his jaw, fingers sliding over ever-smiling lips. Lake snapped his gaze to the beadboard skirting the walls.

"Philip, the guy with the alligator shoes," Knight corrected.

"And the penchant for clapping when he's excited," Lake

added, flustered. He cleared his throat. "We're in Port Rātapu, arguably the most liberal town around. Hooking him up should be easy."

"Careful, Lake," Knight said. "Messing with other people's love lives might backfire."

"They might not have love lives, otherwise."

"Fine," Knight said, laughing. "I was thinking of having a barbecue next weekend. Invite Philip and whoever you'd like. Have a little fun for one afternoon. But don't be surprised if it doesn't work—there might be a reason Philip-with-the-alligator-shoes doesn't have a boyfriend."

2

The following afternoon, Lake swung the Knight's door open, tidied his shoes onto the rack, and paused outside the living room.

Knight stood at the fireplace, head bowed, brows sloped into a frown. Sunlight from the windows printed a large square of light over his T-shirt, jeans, and the heels of his naked feet. Lost in thought, Knight pinched the lily he'd left on the mantelpiece by the stem, shutting his eyes as he breathed in that creamy-clove scent. A weary sigh sagged his shoulders.

Tenderness thumped in Lake's chest. At Knight's fond smile, he pushed into the room.

Knight's head shot up and he clasped his hands behind his back. "Lake."

Lake smiled softly. "You miss your son."

"My son?" Surprise—confusion?—flickered over Knight's face.

Lake gestured to the lily behind him. "You don't have to hide it from me. I like the reminder that you're human."

Knight paused, and returned the lily to the mantelpiece. "All too human, I'm afraid."

"Don't worry. You hide it well."

"That seems the right thing to do." After a beat, Knight looked over at Lake with practiced tolerance. "The barbecue is not until next Sunday. Why are you back?"

"Why do you think I left?" Lake dropped his satchel onto the armchair and draped himself on his favorite couch. "I promised to help at the food bank. I'd have been here an hour ago, but Philip needed a ride home. He hates being in his big empty apartment. He was reluctant to get out of the car."

"And you think the apartment is the reason?"

"I invited him to the barbecue—you should have seen how fast he lit up."

Knight's lips rolled into a half-grin, yet his voice resonated boredom. "I can imagine. Why are you back?"

A yawn pulled at Lake, deep in his chest. It had been a long day on little sleep. "You have two guestrooms."

"You have an entire cottage and your father's old distillery."

True. However . . . "Neither feel the same since he passed away."

Knight spoke tentatively, "It's been years . . ."

"Years practically living with you and your son."

Knight narrowed worried eyes on him. "Or years avoiding the past?"

Lake waggled a finger at him, grinning over the lingering pain of losing his dad on the heels of losing his mum. "Shrewd man."

"My son doesn't live here."

"Shrewder still." Lake sighed. "His and Amy's new house isn't the same. I feel like a third wheel."

"That would be an accurate assessment." A pause. "You were a third wheel here, too."

"Yes, but it was easier with you." More comfortable. He could always be completely himself.

Lake fished for the remote on the coffee table, not quite reaching it, but not quite willing to work for it either. He threw Knight a cheeky wink. "I've taken your guest room upstairs. We're sharing a bathroom."

Knight moved to the coffee table and offered him the remote. "Have you considered finding a more permanent living arrangement? Selling your inherited properties?"

Lake took the other end, but Knight didn't let go. Awaiting an answer, of course. "The cottage maybe," Lake admitted, "but the distillery has been in the Lakewood family for generations. Even though it's sitting there unused, it feels wrong to give it up."

Knight released his hold on the remote. "Start with the cottage, then."

"It's an awful lot of organizing—" At Knight's flattening lips, Lake started nodding "—which I will get on to, very, very soon."

If Knight were inanimate, he'd be an actionable item list. Procrastination was uncharted territory to him. He screamed checkbox, and a smarter person would grab the nearest pencil and start checking.

Lake offered up his most charming smile. "And until I get around to it?"

Knight sighed. "The guestroom downstairs has its own bathroom."

"So actually, about that room. I had a thought."

"Why do I suddenly feel anxious?"

Knight plucked up the remarkably preserved lily—all that hairspray, perhaps?—and hiked toward the archway that led to the dining room.

Lake rolled off the couch and skedaddled after him to the open kitchen. Door knobs, light fixtures, faucets, and hinges were all wrought-iron. Everything so charmingly rustic, a horse braying in the background wouldn't have felt out of place.

"Amy's cousin Harry. Early twenties, cute face. Auburn hair and freckles."

"I recall. Very polite, very happy. Danced with his grandmother and his cousin most of the night. Seemed impressed with the wedding ceremony and reception."

"He did love the crostini."

Knight slipped the lily into a miniature vase and side-eyed him. "He wasn't the only one."

"Are there any left?"

Knight set the vase by the vintage water pitcher Lake had encouraged Taylor to buy his dad for Christmas, and opened the pantry. He brought out a crostini platter. "Picked them up this afternoon. If you hadn't turned up uninvited, I'd have tracked you down."

Lake grabbed a baked artichoke and parmesan crostini and moaned into a crunchy bite. "You're the best, Knightly."

"I do try, Emerett."

Lake swallowed at his first name. It wasn't something anyone else used, just Knight, and only on occasion. But when he did . . . it always jolted him.

"What about this Harry, then?"

Lake finished his mouthful. "Right. Well, he's staying with that cousin he danced with."

"Martin."

"Since Harry has decided to stay in town, he's worried about wearing out his welcome sleeping on Martin's couch."

"You think I should offer him one of my rooms?"

"He is your nephew-in-law."

Knight eyed him closely, gaze rolling over Lake like a shiver. "Why do you want him here, Lake?"

Lake looked everywhere but at Knight. "Just looking out for Taylor's new family."

Knight barked out a laugh. "This is about that romantic meddling."

"These crostini are epic."

Garfield rounded the wooden recipe stand with a heavy purr, and Knight caught her before she fished for some crostini of her own. He tucked her against his chest and patted her with a wry smile at Lake. "I suppose if you're here, it'll be good to have constant distraction."

Crumbs tumbled out of his mouth. "I'm not that bad."

"Who said anything about bad?"

Knight's hair and eyes were like wet wood in spring. He exuded freshness. All those brisk morning walks he took. The outdoor air clung to him.

Usually, it was exceptionally easy to breathe around him. Not so much now.

Garfield jumped from Knight's arms, landing on the tiled floor with a *kathump*.

Their gazes unlatched, and Lake frowned. Knight always had a coolly powerful presence, but with Taylor between them, Lake had been buffered from his full magnificent force. It was . . . was . . .

Something to get used to. "So, Harry can stay?"

"Harry can stay."

"Excellent." Lake clasped Knight's shoulder and squeezed, fingertips grazing his warm neck. "He's arriving at six."

A resigned chuckle vibrated through his palm. "Whatever schemes you have in mind, remember: choosing is better than being chosen for."

F or the first time, a curious shyness heated Lake's neck as he greeted Knight's colleagues and neighbors. He had never attended one of these barbecues without Taylor, and Knight's gaze on him from the honeysuckle-choked gazebo where he manned the grill didn't ease his shyness.

Lake straightened his shoulders and plucked his heat-soaked T-shirt from his chest. He was no feeble man, and Knight had fun friends. Easy to chat with.

Knight flipped a burger, but his focus never wavered from Lake.

A funny little shiver skipped through Lake's body, pooling in the soles of his feet. Each step in his flip flops riddled him with electricity, and he quashed a horrifyingly squeaky laugh. Knight was far too curious about Lake's matchmaking plans with Harry and Phillip. That's all.

Well keep watching, Knight. He'd have them falling for one another before the last hamburger was grilled.

Now, where was Harry? Philip would be arriving any moment.

Ah, there on the bench in the shade, smearing copious amounts of sunscreen over his face. Close to the gazebo and Knight's prying gaze. Another silly shiver.

Nothing for it but to forge ahead, prove his magic meddling abilities.

Lake threaded through guests and slung himself on the worn slats next to Harry, on the side that offered the best view of Knight. He liked reading the man's expressions, being aware of what he might be thinking.

He dragged his gaze back to Harry. "Any more sunscreen, and you'll mask all your cute freckles."

Harry chortled. "You're the second person to call my freckles cute."

"Who was the first?"

Harry blushed—impossible to see through the sunscreen, but his neck looked close to catching fire. "Martin, when he drove us back to his place after Taylor's wedding."

Harry had been staying in Knight's guestroom for a week. His grandma came up in conversation a lot, and so did Martin, which said a lot about his character.

Cute, and he cared about family. A sweet, ceaselessly happy guy who liked everyone. A good guy.

Perfect for Philip.

"Your cousin's right. They're one of your standout features, and you should totally flaunt them."

"I'm not really the flaunting kind. And if I don't wear SPF 50, I crisp in minutes."

Lake hummed in sympathy, and then grinned. Across the yard, Philip emerged from the patio door. God, he must be dying in a long-sleeved button-down and jeans. They looked good on him, though. Pity about the turquoise alligator shoes.

Still, Harry was the type to overlook odd details, notably the gallons of polish Philip must have used.

"Philip, over here!"

Philip's gaze tracked him and his step quickened.

Nervous excitement churned in Lake's gut, and he glanced over at Knight, who shook his head with wry amusement.

Lake stirred restlessly on the bench, then returned his attention to Harry.

" . . . Martin's a big reader—me, not so much. But I love

movies, and I left a list of classics for him to watch, starting with *Mansfield Park*. Gosh, I hope he likes it. Not everyone likes it, what with the cousins marrying . . ." He bit his lip. "It's a pity he couldn't come today. I hope he's not *too* sick. Maybe I should text him."

Harry dug into his shorts' pocket and Lake rested a hand on his elbow. "Hold that thought, Harry." Lake leaped to his feet and raised his arm for a hug as Philip approached.

Philip gripped him firmly back with a joyful hello. Such enthusiasm. He'd fit nicely with happy Harry.

Lake pulled back. "Philip, this is Harry, a friend of mine. An actor."

Harry laughed nervously. "A hopeful actor."

Philip clapped. "Nice. A lot of acting opportunities around here, is there?"

"I'm from Wellington, but my grandma lives in Port Rātapu. And Martin . . ."

Lake clasped Philip on the shoulder. "Sit down, I'll get us drinks."

Grinning enthusiastically at Lake, Philip immediately sat and busied himself in conversation with Harry.

Good start. Very good start.

Lake smirked at Knight as he picked his way over the stone path to the gazebo.

"The drinks station is under the apple tree," Knight said.

He'd overheard it all, then.

Lake snuck nearer to Knight until the grill blasted heat at his front; he felt every miniscule shift Knight made as he flipped his burgers. "Not right away," he murmured under his breath. "Gotta give them time. Do you think they can see me hiding?"

Knight stepped one foot back and pivoted toward him. Another potent wave of heat blazed into Lake, and that squeaky laugh reappeared. He cleared his throat. "That should do it, thanks."

Knight shook his head. "Dare I ask how it's going?"

"I don't know what new info you need, you've been watching everything."

Knight turned an amused grin toward the grill. "Harry really loves his cousin."

Lake snorted. "It's nice that he looks up to Martin, but I think this barbecue is a good thing for him. He needs more friends."

"Looks up to? Hmmm."

"I'm afraid to tell him I don't remember Martin from the wedding."

"Slightly larger man, very neat. Cowlick."

"Doesn't ring a bell. Did you talk to him?"

"I did. He asked me some sensible investment questions." Knight never used that impressed tone regarding Lake. It prickled to hear it now. Who *was* this Martin? "He'll go far in life," Knight decided.

"How can you know that? You can't have spoken to him very long."

"An enjoyable half hour."

"When? I didn't see you chatting with anyone that long. I'm sure I'd have noticed."

"You always have had a good radar for my whereabouts."

The base of Lake's throat flushed. "It's called survival instinct." He pulled his ear, staring at the grill. "Something you need when climbing the trellis into your best friend's room and sneaking to casinos."

"You were both nineteen, and Taylor is sensible. You did nothing that I wasn't aware of."

Lake gaped. "What about the time on his eighteenth—"

"You flew him to Auckland for a night."

"Easter, the year before—"

"You brought home a stolen chicken and hid it in the shed."

"University graduation—"

"I replaced the vase."

Lake smiled grimly. "That's frightening. How on earth do you tolerate me?"

"Practice."

Lake grinned, grabbed a bun, and pried it open with his thumbs. "Thirty minutes with Martin and you know he'll go far in life? No one can judge a man that quickly."

"Can't *you*? Isn't that why Harry's your new best friend?"

"He's not my best friend. Not like your son." Lake frowned. "And I don't know everything about Harry. I just have a good feeling."

"As I have with Martin."

Lake nudged Knight with his arm, eliciting a twinkle-eyed laugh. "You're so curiously annoying."

Knight slipped a sizzling hamburger inside Lake's bun and met his eyes. "You're so charmingly blind."

A series of *dings* burst from Knight's pocket. Knight set the spatula down and pulled out his phone. He smiled, and Lake wanted him to lift that smile over the phone to him.

"Who's messaging you? Can't be Taylor, or my phone would have dinged too."

"Taylor might message me outside our group chat, Lake."

"Did he?"

"No."

Lake tried to peer at Knight's phone, but Knight held it against his chest.

Lake gasped. "Is it a man? Your secret lover?"

"A man, yes. My secret lover?" Knight's gaze grew more impatient than usual. "Not him."

"I'll find a way to your phone, Knight. Telling me now would make this easier on both of us."

Knight snorted. "It's Josh."

"Josh from down the street? Josh with the curly blue hair? Josh who's at Oxford?"

"Josh, who *graduated* from Oxford."

"Oxford?" came another voice behind him. Lake shifted to the side—Cameron, their neighbor. He was a regular at Knight's barbecues and brunches; twenty-five, freakishly good-looking, with thick-rimmed glasses and an unfortunate taste in clothes. Knight, wearing a cooking apron, looked like a fashion God next to Cameron.

"Are you talking about Josh?" Cameron asked, trying to push up his glasses while holding two drinks. "Did he invite you to his coming home party?"

Knight flashed his phone. "He did."

"He didn't invite me." Lake scowled and took a large bite of his burger.

"To be fair, Lake," Knight said, "you hogged the karaoke machine at his farewell. And his high school ex ended up kissing you . . ."

"I did not ask for that kiss."

"Nevertheless."

Lake swallowed another ripped bite and grinned. "If Josh is having a party, I'm going. One of you will take me as your date."

Knight cleared his throat. "Please tell me one of those drinks is for me, Cameron?"

Cameron handed one over; Knight thanked him and sipped, glancing at Lake.

"Cameron is about to update me on my investment in his and his brother's channel. He's hoping to recreate famous period dramas with a gay-romance slant."

"Including Jane Austen's works. My favorites." Cameron added with a bright chuckle, "'The person, be it gentleman or lady, who has not pleasure in a good novel, must be intolerably stupid.'" An expectant stare. If he was waiting for Lake to guess what book that came from . . .

Cameron shrugged. "Northanger Abbey."

The guy's passion for Austen had always been palpable. Now that he'd teamed up with his older brother to produce LGBTQ+ period-dramas, his dream was within reach.

Cameron straightened his glasses. "Everything is progressing nicely except for the hitch in location."

Lake smiled widely and inched away. About time he got back to his goal, anyway. . . . He dropped by the drinks station, and quietly returned to Harry and Philip—wow those shoes were shiny!

Huddled close on the bench, Philip was nodding to Harry's story about . . . *Martin*.

Lake refrained from palming his forehead. What was his fascination with the man? It was almost like Harry was—

Oh God.

Harry had a crush on his cousin.

Heated from scalp to toe, he peered over at Knight. *That*'s what he'd meant when he said Lake was blind.

Knight did a doubletake, realizing Lake had figured it out.

Great. No doubt he'd hear more of Knight's thoughts regarding his failure to observe crucial details later.

Which wasn't the rule, dammit. Lake just missed this *one* connection. That's all.

He studied Harry's enthusiastic retelling, hands waving about.

So. Harry *like*-liked his cousin. That was . . . well, to each their own.

But . . .

Perhaps Harry fixated on Martin because he didn't know any other gay men?

Maybe meeting Philip would show him there were more

fish in the sea. Good idea for Harry to see the extent of the buffet before he filled his plate with the first dish he saw.

Philip spotted Lake and beamed. "Lake, thanks for the drinks. Harry was just telling me the funniest story about a tortoise."

Harry's neck brightened, and Philip's smile grew.

Those were some happy details.

Lake winked at Philip as he passed him a beer. Give him a couple of weeks. He'd make sure Philip wasn't alone in his big apartment for long.

4

Parked outside Knight's picket-fenced yard after clocking eight hours editing a boring toothpaste commercial, Lake scrolled through the most recent volley of honeymoon pictures.

He paused on Taylor and Amy gazing dreamily at one another at the Arc de Triomphe.

He should be responding with heart-eyed emojis, not swallowing the tightness in his throat because he missed Taylor.

No, that was selfish of him. Amy was wonderful; she made Taylor happy.

Maybe Taylor's absence wasn't the problem.

Lake scrubbed his hands over his face and groaned. Did he want love for *himself*?

"Stop it."

Much more rewarding helping others fall in love. Muddling about trying to figure it out for himself never worked. He lacked the necessary objectivity.

Sunshine streamed through the windshield, cooking Lake in his semi-formal workwear. He dragged himself and his silly heartache into the house and moped into the dining room, where Knight had taken to working all week. He instantly felt better. Lake thrived on other people's energy, and Knight exuded quiet, calm energy.

"There's a carafe of chilled water in the fridge for after your run," Knight said, without looking up from his laptop.

"You did that for me?"

Knight scrutinized his screen. "Flatter yourself if you like, Lake. But it's mostly for my benefit."

Quiet, calm, deeply honest energy.

Lake cracked a grin—the first all day. "Yours?"

Knight gave Lake a swift sideways glance, brown eyes piercing him with a dose of unfamiliar self-consciousness. "I can't stand watching you suck water straight from the faucet."

"Tastes better like that."

Lake stood still, gripping his shoulder bag, staring at Knight purposefully tapping at his keyboard. A prominent vein ran over the back of each large hand to agile fingers. Agile and practiced and—

He pivoted away.

God, he needed a run.

"You might want to convince Harry to go with you," Knight called after him as he headed upstairs. "He hasn't left his room all day."

Lake changed course and approached the guest bedroom. He knocked on the paneling. "Harry?"

A thump sounded—along with an *oof*—and then the door opened, sucking at the hallway air.

Harry wore an oversized hoodie and jeans. He'd parted his hair down the middle and sprayed himself with an ounce too much peppery cologne. "Yeah?"

Lake blinked at him. "What are you doing?"

"Practicing my comedic monologues for auditions."

"You certainly look comedic. You've been doing that all day?"

An eager nod.

Knight was right. No surprise there.

"Exchange the crime you're wearing for some running gear. We're leaving in five."

"Oh, I don't actually run. That is, I've never really tried." Harry gulped, nodding with forced enthusiasm. "No time like the present?"

When they'd both changed, Lake ushered Harry toward

the front door.

The bell chimed while they were tightening their laces, ringing in Lake's sensitive ears.

He opened the door to a man poised to press the buzzer again. Rounded face gently framed by a cowlick and wavy blond locks, and shy but attentive eyes.

A breathy gasp came from behind Lake, and Harry lurched to his side.

So this must be Martin.

Forget hellos. Martin's gaze strayed to Harry and settled there. Delight shone in his eyes, and Martin found his voice. "Hey, Harry."

Harry stepped onto the threshold and embraced him. "What are you doing here?"

Martin pulled back with a glance at Lake and patted the laptop bag slung over his shoulder. "Knightly invited me. He's giving me a tutorial in setting up stock funds."

"How are you feeling?" Harry's gaze roamed fastidiously over Martin's face for signs of lingering illness.

"Feeling? Oh, I didn't make the barbecue. I had a . . . migraine."

Martin's cheek twitched. Lying.

Lake frowned. This was not good. Last year, he'd dated a liar, and their relationship had quickly spiraled out of control. Taylor, away with Amy, had ended up calling his dad in the middle of the night to collect Lake from the police station after he'd been framed for burglary.

Lake wasn't easily frightened, but that cool fall night he'd cried in Knight's arms. On brisk evenings since, he recalled Knight's firm strokes along his back and his carefully-worded concern in Lake's ear like a ticklish ghost.

". . . did you watch *Mansfield Park*?" Harry asked, bouncing on the balls of his feet, sounding as excited about Austen as Cameron was.

"No," Martin said, grimacing. "Not yet."

Harry stopped bouncing. "Maybe another time."

Lake hated that Harry was bummed about it, but he was convinced he could do better than dating a liar and ending up in a steel holding cell.

He hooked an arm around Harry's and urged him past Martin. "We're off for a run. Knight's in the kitchen."

Harry let out a surprised 'bye' and watched over his shoulder as Martin entered the house.

Lake didn't let him go until the gate latched shut behind them.

Their run was short and labored, and Lake spent most of it worried that Harry might collapse.

But A+ for effort. He admired Harry's diligence.

When they returned home, Martin and Knight had vacated the kitchen for the back yard, and Lake and Harry went to their respective bathrooms and showered.

Freshened, Lake trundled downstairs to Harry, who'd tied his towel around his head.

Harry poured them water from the carafe, leaned against the counter, and smiled shyly. He'd been far too puffed to chat on their run, but Lake had felt his burning need to.

"So, what'd you think of Martin?"

Lake lifted his chilled glass, and shrugged. "He barely spoke."

"Come on . . . you have eyes. He's gorgeous, right?"

"You know what struck me? For close relatives, you don't look anything alike."

Harry mumbled into a sip. "He takes more after his dad, I guess."

"Are you close with your uncle?"

Harry frowned. "You think the cousin thing is wrong, then?"

Lake hesitated. Harry was soft-hearted and liked to please,

but he certainly wasn't stupid. The truth was, Lake couldn't quite shake how forbidden it felt.

On the other hand, he was a firm believer in love is love. "Not wrong, exactly. But you'd need to make sure you both feel the same. There will be some who won't like it."

Harry's shoulders sagged and he blinked rapidly.

Lake strangled his water glass and cleared the sympathetic lump in his throat. He felt for Harry, but he was young. How would his soft heart cope exposed to harsh criticism? Family rejection? "Maybe open yourself to other possibilities? If nothing compares to what you feel for Martin . . . Just be sure first?"

Harry nodded, towel slipping. "You're right. But Martin is special. He's clever and good. He cares about his family, and he's sensible about his career and finances. He's a younger Knightly. Maybe not quite Knightly, but very good."

Lake chuckled. "Unfair to compare him with Knight. No one's as good as he is."

"Why doesn't he have a partner?" Harry said in a low voice, like he might be overheard. "He's the whole package. Someone should snap him up."

"When you're that good looking and self-sufficient, you get to do the snapping. I bet no one's good enough." Lake's phone vibrated in his pocket and he pulled it free. "It's from Philip." Lake grinned. "'I liked Sunday, seeing you, meeting your friend.'"

Harry's towel fell off his head and he raced to retrieve it. "Me?"

"You should have traded numbers."

"Oh. Really? I should have?"

"He was totally into you."

"He was?"

"Good looking guy too, don't'cha think?"

Harry almost dropped his bundled towel again. "Um . . . yep. Philip was nice."

Lake read the text again. It seemed like Philip was fishing for clues that Harry had enjoyed meeting him too.

Lake: Want to join us for a movie tonight?

Philip: Harry will be there too?

Lake suppressed a surge of premature triumph. "He sounds eager."

Harry blushed, and Lake's grin deepened as he replied. He'd find an excuse to bail at the last minute. Leave the two alone.

Philip: I wish I could! Would be great to see you, but my boss just requested I stay late. Another time?

"Disappointing."

Harry agreed, but cheerfully picked up when Martin and Knight emerged from the back yard.

Martin waved awkwardly to Harry, who eyed him longingly from the kitchen. He slung his laptop bag over his shoulder, thanked Knight again for his help, and left.

Harry raced after him, and Lake wasn't sure he liked it.

Knight, wearing a beetle-brown T-shirt that matched his hair and eyes, steadied a cautioning look at him from across the room as if he knew what judgmental thoughts rocketed through his mind. Lake felt appropriately chastised.

Not that he'd ever admit that to Knight.

"So, Knight . . ."

"Lake . . ."

Lake lifted his glass of carafe water, winked, and downed it. "Why are you single?"

5

Knight sat quietly in the car next to Lake, perhaps confused that Lake had invited himself. He couldn't say exactly why he'd done it, but after chasing Garfield into her carrier, it seemed logical for him to attend her annual checkup . . . in case he had to help Knight again.

Finding a parking space was a pain in the ass until Lake suggested his dad's—*his*—distillery grounds. The fern-dense valley dipping behind the vet clinic led to a few hidden Port Rātapu treasures—a huge Victorian manse fenced in stone and shrouded with native bush, a large pristine estate on the far end near the coast, and their destination: a rundown brick warehouse with boarded windows, wildly growing vines, and a peeling Lakewood Bourbon sign.

The car stopped, and Lake fought a wild ache. He remembered playing outside that detached shed next to the tree. Remembered piggyback rides and tours through his dad's struggling but beloved distillery.

He slicked on a smile and quickly climbed out of the car with his shoulder bag.

The smell. So familiar. All that dank brick and dust and kōwhai pollen.

Knight studied him over the roof of the car.

Lake pivoted away from his inheritance and strode down a long gravel path to the main street.

Knight followed, hefting the carrier. Garfield mewled at the stray droplets of rain leaking through the air vents, the swaying motion, and the unfairness of being dragged from the comfort of home.

Lake agreed. "I make a similar whine every day I head to work."

Knight glanced at him. "Have you thought about changing jobs?"

"I think about it a lot." A sneaky raindrop weaseled under Lake's collar. "Another thing for the to-do list."

"If you ever need help . . ."

"You'd definitely be the one I ask." Lake meant that from every crevice of his heart. "Even before Taylor."

Knight beheld him with a quiet frown that made Lake swallow.

"You have more experience," Lake explained, although that didn't feel entirely honest.

They walked on, curious silence once more descending over Knight. His strong nose, heavy eyebrows, that mouth that curled into a grim smile. What was he thinking?

Knight had been suffering in this contemplation since Lake had asked why he was single. God, he almost wished he could take it back.

Except . . .

Maybe Knight needed a reminder to open himself up to the possibility of meeting someone.

Knight caught Lake staring, and shivery electricity jolted through him from the back of his nose to the balls of his feet.

Beautiful shops lined the street. Tranquil Café, Poise Art Gallery, the barber shop . . .

He couldn't take it anymore. "What's on your mind?"

Knight answered swiftly, "I have a bad feeling about you meddling in Harry's love life."

Lake frowned. Not what he'd been expecting. "A bad feeling? Why?"

"You have a compelling personality, Lake. People like to have your attention."

"What's wrong with that? I'm giving Harry attention."

"Just be careful."

Lake straightened, gait lengthening. "Harry and I are friends. I'm helping him find romance."

Knight easily matched his step. "You mean well. You always do."

"What does *that* mean?"

Knight didn't hold back. "You get excited about a project, do copious research, and dream how amazing it will turn out. Remember your photographer phase? You bought a two-thousand-dollar camera, stands, lighting gear. You turned my gazebo into a set."

"I still use that camera."

Knight raised a brow.

"I do!"

"Is that why it's clogging up my attic?"

Dammit. "That was *one* project."

"I also remember your chef phase—though I thank you for leaving those knives behind—and then there was the time you rearranged all of my bookshelves into alphabetical order, asked me what each book meant to me, and vowed to read every one of them."

Lake winced.

Knight's expression softened. "I know in your heart you really *think* you'll follow through with your plans."

"I follow through with my plans."

"How did you like *Moby Dick*?"

"The title was intriguing."

"And the rest?"

"It's not my fault you like boring books!" Lake cast him an indignant scowl. "Fine, I didn't read any of your favorite reads, and maybe a few other projects never saw the light of day, but that doesn't mean I'll get impatient and abandon Harry."

"I don't want to see anyone hurt."

"Do you always think the worst of me?"

An astounded laugh barked out of Knight. "No. I really don't."

Lake didn't need more confirmation than that, but . . . He halted in the middle of the sidewalk. "Tell me something good then."

Knight set the carrier down and stepped close to Lake. Fingers cupped his jaw and a thumb tapped against the edge of Lake's mouth. "This charming smile you're giving me while fishing for compliments." Fondness beamed in Knight's eyes, then he dropped his hand and cleared his throat. "Look, Harry is the kind of guy who'd follow you off a cliff. So just watch where you're walking, okay?"

Lake waved a dismissive hand, still feeling the heat of Knight's thumb on his lips. "Go back to complimenting me. Nice smile. Anything else?"

Knight shook his head in disbelief. "You know you're attractive."

"Attractive? From someone who actually read all those books, I expect better diction than *attractive*."

Knight laughed. "Fine. Beautiful."

"Still think you can do better."

Knight held his gaze. "The most beautiful man I've met." He picked up Garfield's carrier and walked like he hadn't started punching butterflies into Lake's chest. "I love how rarely you let your looks get to your head. You consider them a mild inconvenience, even."

He was being honest, that's all. Knight wasn't the kind of man to resist empirical truths, and Lake had pushed him to state the obvious. Not that he thought himself the most beautiful man, but he knew he looked good—many had said so before.

But no-one else's words had knocked him so off-center.

"Many wonderful adjectives describe you, Lake, but don't derail this conversation. Will you be careful with Harry?"

Lake took three long rain-scented gulps. "I'll be careful if you promise to keep your thoughts to yourself."

"As long as I see you being careful, I will keep my thoughts to myself."

Lake laughed. "You're ridiculously frustrating to talk to. Maybe that's why you're single."

"Ditto."

Rain spilled from the sky. Lake pulled out the umbrella he kept in his bag, and opened it above them. They huddled close, Garfield crammed between them, and their gazes caught. Knight's sparkled with good humor, and it yanked a grin from Lake. He shook his head. "What will become of us?"

6

Lake invited Philip to dinner during their volunteer shift. He'd meant for him to come over later that night, but after they'd finished their shift, Philip followed him to his car and buckled himself in.

On the drive home, Philip fished after who else would be there, and Lake bit down on a grin. One would have to be clueless not to see how into Harry Philip was.

Lake helloed the house as they entered, and found Harry pacing the lounge with the phone to his ear and Knight making a crashing sound in the kitchen.

Knight darted his gaze away from them and crouched to a watering can gushing liquid over the floorboards.

Had he been taken aback by Philip? Lake should've given him a heads up, but he also hadn't expected Philip to hop into his car right away.

Harry waved brightly, and Philip whispered in Lake's ear.

"Harry really lights up around you. I get it. You're generous and kind, and . . ." Philip swallowed thickly.

"He's an easy guy to hang with." Lake shrugged.

Philip rocked back on his heels and nodded vigorously. "Totally. Is he wearing your clothes?" Harry rocked a tight pair of jeans and a slim-fitting T-shirt that made his blue eyes pop. "It's a very"—Philip looked back at Lake—"hot look."

Lake donned a self-congratulatory grin. "Yeah."

Philip's brow quirked and he smiled, then shifted, like he wanted to share another secret. Lake dipped his head forward, ready for Philip to admit that he was into Harry but nervous to ask him out.

Harry ended his phone call with a groan. "What's wrong?" Lake asked.

"My agent says I need better head shots for my portfolio. Actually, one head shot and one freestyle picture."

Lake might have ditched most of the projects he started, but each had taught him a skill. This was a problem Lake could solve. And on the heels of his conversation with Knight, it was a problem he wanted to solve.

As if he sensed Lake's smug look, Knight glanced over from where he was watering his flowering houseplants and aloe vera. Their eyes met with that strangely addictive, illicit zing.

Would he ever get used to the force of Knight's looks?

He ripped his focus back to Harry, palming his hips. "Let's do it."

Harry wrecked his hair with his fingers. "I can't afford a professional photographer."

Knight rang out a disbelieving laugh. "Good lord." He addressed Harry. "Lake has all the equipment needed to take a professional shot."

Not the same as saying Lake *could* take a professional shot, Knight's doubtful look said.

Determination bubbled in his chest. "I'll take the best shots you've ever seen."

Philip clapped gleefully.

Harry bit his lip. "Now?"

"Why not? It's good weather, approaching the golden hour."

"I've got to darken my eyes." Harry gulped and shot out the room.

Lake smiled cheekily at Knight. "Will you help me gather the gear from the attic?"

"From a dark, tight space?" Philip said, breath-smellingly close to his side. "I'd love to help you."

"Unnecessary." Knight's expression tightened. "It's a mess up there, and some boards can't be stepped on. Lake and I will get everything as soon as I finish watering."

Lake turned to find Philip's teeth flashing before his face.

"I bet you'll take the perfect picture of Harry. You're good at everything."

"Well, not everything. But this shouldn't be hard. Harry's a cute guy with a stunning face, especially those freckles."

"I'm sure you'll capture him from his best angle."

"Hopefully, but I'm a little worried that Harry is nervous about posing. He bolted from the room so fast."

"I can help relax him." Philip slid a hand over Lake's shoulder and squeezed. "I'm really good at massaging—"

Knight ducked through the arch, smothering a cough. "The watering can wait. Let's go."

Lake hoofed after Knight, tossing over his shoulder to Philip, "Start calming Harry. I'll meet you at the gazebo."

Lake followed Knight up a narrow, foldaway ladder into the darkness of the attic. Light beamed from Knight's phone, casting a glow over mountains of boxes. Beams creaked as they picked their way across the crammed space.

"Sorry about the lack of warning about our guests," Lake said. "I'll cook. What do you want?"

"Anything you like, as long as it comes with a side of Tylenol."

"What's the Tylenol for?"

"Philip. Possibly Harry. Definitely you."

"Me?"

A dry chuckle. "Please don't pretend to have no idea."

The surprise visit. His meddling, which Knight had emphatically warned him about. A slither of guilt itched in his belly.

Knight spotted his camera gear. "If you take your camera, I'll bring the rest."

Lake sat on a steel-hinged crate. "Mind if we stay up here a few minutes?"

Knight glanced at him. "Why?"

"I want Philip and Harry to bond without us."

Knight perched on a wooden crate next to him and let out a weary laugh. "I don't think they'll bond as well as you think they will."

Lake waved a dismissive hand. "You've spent the better part of the last seven years single. What do you know about bonding? Now, what do you think, navy bowtie for their big day?"

"Forest green, but there won't be a big day. And I haven't been a monk. There've been opportunities."

Their legs bumped every other exhale. "Why didn't you take them?"

"I wasn't thrilled with any of the matches."

"None?"

"I have a problem."

Lake cupped his mouth, shielding a horrified whisper. "Down there?"

"And I'm leaving." Knight stood, and Lake hooked a finger in the beltloop of his jeans and steered him back down. His finger stayed nestled around that strip of denim.

"Stay. I'm sorry. I mean, it's okay if it's not working. There are pills for that."

Knight shook his head; his jaw twitched as if caught between a laugh and a groan. "I'm close to clobbering you with your camera."

"I'm serious."

"That's why I'm so close." Knight shifted, knees angling toward Lake. Lake's finger fell from the belt loop. Brown eyes flashed in the muted light. "There's nothing dysfunctional about my cock."

The word sizzled through Lake, pooling in his crotch. It must have been because it was dark. Dark and warm, and they were so close their breaths were knotting.

"Jesus, Knight. I expected 'manhood' or 'member' from you. You shocked me with *cock*."

"I'm sorry. That was inappropriate."

"No, you didn't shock me up here." Lake tapped his head, and then pointed toward his lap. "Shocked me there, if you know what I mean."

Knight's gaze followed his pointed finger. He slammed his eyes closed and breathed in deeply, like he needed extra patience to deal with Lake's nonsense.

A baffling giggle escaped Lake. Hell, it almost seemed like he was nervous. But it was just Knight. Taylor's relentlessly longsuffering dad.

Lake returned to their conversation. "Why didn't any matches work for you?"

Knight inhaled deeply, let it go, and reopened his eyes. He focused on Lake's camera. "I have a picture of the man I want to be with, and no one else comes close."

"The man must be perfect. And well read."

"Trust me, he is neither of those things."

"Sounds like you're talking about a real person?"

Knight hesitated. "I am."

The confirmation prickled. It was just . . . he liked to think he knew all the important things about the Dixons. Lake should have picked up on this secret crush earlier.

Best he pay better attention. He eyed Knight carefully. "I'm sorry, Knight."

"Sorry?"

"He's straight, isn't he? I mean, he has to be."

"He's not straight."

"Who else would turn you down? You have the driest humor this side of the hills."

"Is that all I've got going for me?"

"Now look who's fishing for compliments!"

"Don't act surprised. I like to hear one or two positive things about me from time to time."

"I could tell you sixteen things."

"How highly specific."

Lake smirked. "Well, I read this online article about boyfriends and finding Mr. Right. The short story is that you, Knightly Dixon, are a Mr. Right."

Knight leaned in, whispering with a twitching smile. "And the long story?"

A laugh bubbled up from deep in his gut and poured out of Lake. "The long story is—"

"Lake?" Philip's keen cry drifted up the ladder, and Lake and Knight jerked an inch apart. "You sure you don't need help? Harry and I can carry things."

Knight stood abruptly, and Lake grabbed a tight handful of his camera bag.

Within ten minutes they were set up in the gazebo, a lip-gnawing Harry perched on a stool.

Velvet summer wind breezed over them, and Lake stared at his beefy camera. He knew how to use it, but it had been a while; he was rusty, and he'd rather not let on to Harry or Philip.

He adopted a smile and ordered Harry around. A lot could be said for spirit. Fake it until you make it and all that.

Lake corrected the focus and began snapping, thankful he'd left a loaded battery in the camera bag all those eighteen months ago.

Philip fidgeted at Lake's left, Harry defaulted to biting his lip, and Knight watched quietly from a bench where he'd seated himself with a book.

"Just relax!" Lake called out to Harry. "It's not like we have gawking boyfriends to impress."

Philip's gaze flashed from Harry to Lake with a twinkle. "Not yet, anyway."

Knight snorted.

Lake turned to the bench where Knight was watching them over an open book. "Good read there?"

"Painfully funny scene."

Lake shook his head, smirking.

Philip kept looking over Lake's shoulder, trying to catch glimpses of the display screen. Lake was used to Knight's criticism, but constant ohhh-ing and ahhh-ing was throwing him off his game.

"Philip," Lake said. "Find out what music Harry likes and stream it on your phone?"

Harry's naturally photogenic figure assumed every pose perfectly, but between shots he looked close to shitting himself. Unless that was what blooming romance with Philip looked like?

A minute later, music beat a goofy tune out of Philip's phone. Harry bopped along to it.

"What on earth are we listening to?" Knight said, reading Lake's mind.

Philip cleared his throat and read from his screen. "Tiddlywinks."

The rest of their session revolved around a looping track.

Not quite his thing, but it infused Harry with confidence.

"I'll work on a selection of pictures after dinner," Lake said as they packed the gear away.

Philip clapped. "Can I help you choose the perfect shot?"

Couldn't get enough of Harry, could he?

Lake grinned. "After I've made a pre-selection and cleaned up my favorites."

After I weed out the badly focused and out-of-frame shots.

Dinner was pizza, and a side of Tylenol for Knight. Afterward, Lake suggested Philip and Harry watch a movie while he dabbled with Photoshop.

From the dining table, he had a good view of the lovebirds through the arch; Knight puttered around him, cleaning up.

Lake kicked out the chair beside him and gestured he sit, which made Knight laugh. He finished cleaning and seated himself, the scent of vanilla and oak reminding Lake of their close proximity in the attic.

Lake side-eyed him. "We never finished our conversation."

"By all means. What sixteen things make me Mr. Right?"

Lake snickered. "Why do you think you'd be turned down?"

Knight let out a deep breath. "It's complicated. I'm fairly sure he hasn't any clue of my feelings and it's better that way."

Lake frowned. "Why?"

"Because it can't happen."

"He's off-limits?" Lake gasped. "Is it your boss?" Wasn't Paul married? Wasn't he close to sixty?

"He's in charge, all right."

"Is age difference the problem?"

"Partly, yes. It's a delicate situation involving more than one party."

It *was* Paul then. "What's with all this forbidden romance in the air?"

Why this sudden and immeasurable dislike of Paul?

Paul wouldn't go there. He was happy.

Which left Knight unhappy.

That was the crux of it. Lake didn't care for Knight being lonely. It filled his chest with a hollow ache.

"This is ridiculous," Lake decided. "You're too good-looking to waste away waiting for someone who'll never love you back."

Knight grimaced and leaned back in his chair thoughtfully.

"I should focus on never being loved back, but I confess it's the good-looking comment that snagged me."

"Don't let it snag your modesty. Humility is part of your package."

The flicker in Knight's eye had Lake flushing.

He quickly refocused on his screen, almost relieved when Philip leaped off the couch and sauntered into the dining room.

"What do you think of this one?"

Knight leaned in and inspected it. "Harry looks a little too airbrushed."

"He does not," gasped Philip. "He looks perfect. Look how Lake made his eyes pop."

"What does the actor himself think?" Lake asked, beckoning Harry to look.

Harry grinned. "I look amazing."

"Sure do, your pictures are amazing," Philip said. "Good enough to display in a gallery!"

They scrolled through the other pictures and Harry decided on his favorites.

Lake agreed he chose the best ones. "Now all you need is to print them."

Philip clapped. "There's a proper artist's printshop around the corner from my apartment. Give me the files and I'll get them printed."

Harry blushed, and Lake smiled widely. These guys were totally falling for one another.

He delivered Knight a pointedly smug look, and Knight shook his head. Again.

Whatever.

A year from now, he'd be wearing a forest-green bow tie.

7

Lake pulled off his T-shirt and chucked it to the floor. The last ten hours in his small office clung to him in a musk of stale donuts and sugared coffee. Friday, at last.

He needed a good long soak, followed by a night of hanging out in the lounge, silently warring with Knight over control of the remote.

He withdrew his buzzing phone from his jean's pocket and plunked down on the king-size bed.

Taylor: Two weeks till we're back!

Lake: And . . .?

Taylor: I miss you. Now your ego has been placated, do you remember West?

Lake: West who?

Taylor: My best friend from high-school? Who went to London for two years?

Lake: I forgive you for having a life before me.

Taylor: How has my dad not chucked you out, yet?

Lake: He's holding on by a thread.

Lake: And I suspect he's waiting for me to finish *Moby Dick* that I took from his bookshelf last weekend.

Taylor: How far through are you?

Lake glanced at the fat book on the bedside table.

Lake: It's a whale of a book.

Taylor: 😂

Taylor: Anyway, West emailed me. He wants to meet up when I come back. I figure you and dad will throw a brunch or barbecue, so I'm sending you his number to give him deets.

Lake: Do I have to worry about West coming back into your life?

Taylor: You might be excited. He's smart, gay, and single.

Lake: Give me his number.

Grinning, he leaped off the bed and swung open the bathroom door.

Light hit his eyes, and then blue tiled walls, and then Knight, one hand on the shower door, poised to enter.

Shocked stillness seized Lake; liquid-brown eyes met his, startled.

Lake blinked. "Whoa. I didn't expect . . . so much skin."

Knight looked down at himself. "I'm heading into the shower. I'm supposed to be naked."

A weird laugh jittered out of Lake. He'd never seen Knight with a towel around his waist, let alone the gently muscled lines of his legs, the taut curve of his ass, the broadening planes of his back.

He was gorgeous. And half-hard, like maybe he'd been about to take care of himself during his shower. Lake's feet curled, squealing against the floorboards. God, look away!

Lake gulped. "Sorry, I should have heard the water running."

Knight tucked a towel around his waist. The scant cloth left one brawny thigh exposed. "Eye-contact and apologies generally go together."

Lake jerked his gaze up Knight's powerful body to his enviably calm expression. No shyness, no embarrassment. No humor either.

His eyes were anchored on Lake, reading his every movement—his every thought? Lake wanted to turn the pages for him.

Hope flickered in Knight's eyes and zipped like a current between them.

Lake's breath shortened, and his nipples and balls tightened. That was . . . that was really a sign how long it'd been since he'd been laid. Biological neediness and all that.

Neediness that was obvious, thanks to being shirtless and wearing stretch-fit jeans.

Horrified, Lake ranted, "Shouldn't you be wrinkly?"

"I'm forty-four."

"Shouldn't you be very wrinkly?"

Disbelieving laughter shot out of Knight. "Shouldn't you be looking elsewhere?"

"I can't. Oh my God, I'm checking you out." Lake palmed his eyes and backed out of the bathroom. "Taylor will murder me. Don't you dare tell him. I'll never accidentally look at your insanely hot naked body again."

"Careful, the dresser's behind you." Firm hands grasped

Lake's forearms, pulling him forward, the slide of his fingers rippling through him, electric.

Gently, Knight urged Lake's hands from his eyes.

Their gazes met and Knight's fingers tightened around the heels of his hands for an extended breath.

He let go and a curious ghost-like touch clung to Lake.

"What are you thinking?" Knight asked quietly.

He was close. So close, heat radiated from him.

Lake laughed, then swore. "Will this get awkward? I don't want awkward with you."

"It won't get awkward."

"Are you sure?" Lake pitched his voice to a whisper, "Because I didn't want to look away."

Knight scrubbed a palm over a frustrated smile. His expression steadied, and his voice held its usual rationality. "I was naked, and you liked what you saw. Nothing wrong with that, Lake."

"I was ogling my best friend's dad."

A growly sound came from Knight. "I'm not *your* dad."

"No. No you're not. But . . ."

Knight ran a hand through his hair, and glanced away. "I'm showering, then heading out for the night."

Lake's gaze dropped down Knight's length. *Again.* "Will Paul be there?"

"Yes, actually."

Stupid forbidden crush Paul. "You should wear that sweater Taylor knitted you a few Christmases ago."

"The seaweed-brown monstrosity?"

"That's the one."

Knight rang out a laugh. "Does it disturb you to think of me as a sexual person?"

"It disturbs me thinking you'll bring someone home tonight." Lake jerked a finger at all that muscle. "There's no way you couldn't."

"It's a work gathering. I'll endeavor to keep it professional."

Lake let out a relieved breath. "Thanks."

A contemplative frown crossed Knight's face, and he scrubbed a hand over the slight stubble on his jaw. "Right." He twisted on his heel. "Shower."

"I'll jump in after you."

Knight chuckled, moving into the bathroom. "I'll be sure to empty the warm water."

Flushing, Lake shut the door between them. "Good idea."

Faint laughter followed.

Lake jerked into a shirt, pushed open his window, and sat on the wide sill. Breezes did little to cool his embarrassment and nothing to erase the images of naked Knight, showering. More than showering . . .

A different man, and Lake would have shrugged the moment off, but after seven years knowing someone, seeing them naked felt potent.

Weighted.

Disconcerting.

A knock came at the door. How long had he been daydreaming?

He was not ready to see Knight again. He eyed the trellis descending from his room to the yard and swung his legs over the sill.

His door parted an inch and Lake almost leaped.

Harry's voice sailed into the room. "Lake? Do you have a moment?"

Christ. Just Harry. "You scared me."

"Sorry," Harry said, grinning. "Can I come in? I need your advice."

Lake waved him in and swung back into the room. "Advice?"

"About a boy."

Lake perked. "Spill."

"I kind of bumped into him between auditions yesterday, and he asked me to lunch. We talked forever, way past his lunch hour. It was so easy being with him, and he told me he misses me, even though it hasn't been long."

How serendipitous! "Philip finally spat it out?"

Harry shook his head, laughing. "Not Philip, *Martin*."

Lake frowned. "Martin?"

Harry's smile ate up his face. "I mean, I know lunch wasn't planned, but it counts as a date, right?"

"He might have asked because it was lunchtime and it might have been easy to talk because you're family."

"Oh." Harry's shoulders fell an inch. "Maybe, yeah."

"I mean, I wouldn't rush to interpret his feelings after one lunch date."

Harry slapped a hand on his pocket and hurriedly withdrew his phone. He waved it. "Speak of the devil." Harry read the text. "He says he enjoyed lunch and wants to know if I can come for dinner tomorrow." He looked up. "That sounds like a date, doesn't it?"

Lake searched for the most delicate way to disagree. "I don't know. Maybe he means him and your grandma?"

"Oh. I'll ask."

Before Lake could stop him, Harry tapped out a text.

They waited impatiently for Martin's response, while Lake tried to tamp down any weirdness.

The phone buzzed, and Harry read aloud, "Hoping it'll be just us." His eyes blazed with hope. "Surely that means something?"

Lake hummed. "Maybe. Maybe not."

"Oh, here's another message." Harry cleared his throat. "'I cleared out my study and made it into a spare room. If you want to stay with me again?' What do I do, Lake?"

"Answer him."

"And say what?"

Lake threw up his hands. "No, you have to decide that."

"You think it's a big leap. You think I should focus on Philip?"

"You're the only one who can look into your heart, Harry."

Harry bit his lip. "I mean, every time I look at Martin it feels like I'm swallowing a live wire. But, Philip is attractive too. And super nice, and no one in my family would object . . ."

Harry needed to stop biting his lip or it would come off.

"I mean," Lake blurted, "if you have any doubt, that might indicate your real feelings."

Harry's frame sagged and he dropped onto Lake's bed. "I shouldn't hesitate if Martin is the one."

Lake sat next to Harry and sympathetically patted his leg.

Harry threw himself back and stared at the ceiling. "Besides, he might be acting polite with the room. The dinner too. Maybe he wants us to be better cousins!"

Lake cringed. "Dinner could have ended traumatically."

Harry groaned into his hands. "You're right. How mortifying."

"I know a thing or two about mortifying." Flushing, Lake forced Knight's naked image from his mind. "Wouldn't recommend."

Harry chortle-groaned. "I have to turn down the room."

"I think you're right. Also, I'd be sad if you left."

Harry sat up. "I'd have been sad too. You're the best." He stared at his phone. "Martin's a lovely guy. I'd go to dinner as family, too. But it might hurt. What should I say?"

"Tell him you already have plans. Say thanks for the room, but you're nicely settled here."

Harry started typing, and deleting, and typing again, until Lake opened his hand.

A relieved sigh fled Harry's mouth and he handed over the phone.

Lake sent off a text, and Harry dropped his head on Lake's shoulder. "Has he read it yet?"

Lake checked. "Yes."

"Is he answering?"

"No."

"Does that mean he's upset?"

"Or he's in the middle of a conversation with your grandma. Give him time." Lake found his phone and scrolled to a message from Philip. He waved a shot of Harry's pictures fanned out on a kitchen counter. "Look who got your pictures printed!"

"That was really nice of him."

"Well, he's into you."

Harry smiled.

8

Lake tossed and turned under twisted sheets, unable to rid himself of images of Knight. His body tingled all over, strung taut with pent energy, and . . . Christ.

He gave in to the pleasure of a slick hand.

Some of his tension abated, but it was only *after* Knight returned home—alone—that he succumbed to sleep.

Lake woke freshened, curious to find out about Knight's work gathering. He wouldn't dwell on past embarrassments, and Knight had probably forgotten about it. That whole moment was a blip. Something they'd recall later—much later —and laugh about.

Dressed in shorts and a slim-fit polo, Lake trotted downstairs, *Moby Dick* tucked under his arm. He slung himself on the firm armchair.

At the sound of Knight's heavy footsteps creaking the wooden stairs, Lake lifted his book so the cover was visible and peeked over the top. Knight breezed in with a waft of aftershave—smooth-jawed and crisply dressed in navy chino shorts, a short-sleeved button up, and brown ankle socks—and strode past him. Calves flexed, and reflected light caught on the delicate skin at his ankle.

Lake shifted the book, read another sentence, and guffawed.

Another peek. Knight glanced in his direction with a murmured "morning," before ducking into the dining room.

Lake followed him, reading the whole way.

A shadow landed over the pages, but Lake continued to read.

"Could you be any more obvious?"

He feigned innocence. "What?"

A blank look. "You're angling for praise."

Lake couldn't hold back a grin. He snapped the book shut, set it on the counter, and jumped up next to it. Knight veered around his swinging legs.

"It's a fight to turn pages. Praise would be nice."

Knight poured water into the kettle. "When you've read Shakespeare, Bacon, Austen, and Christie, I'll consider it."

Of course. "Bacon sounds good."

"*The Wisdom of Ancients.*"

"Especially with a side of eggs."

Knight gave him a withering look, but Lake caught his lips hitching as he busied himself making coffee.

Lake's heels rhythmically bumped against the cupboards. "So. How was Paul last night?"

Knight paused, a heaped tablespoon of coffee hovering over a filter cup. "There is nothing between me and Paul."

"Good." At Knight's gently raised brow, Lake cleared his throat and added, "I would have to think less of you, otherwise."

Knight switched on the machine. "I should hope so."

"I don't like the idea of thinking less of you."

"Glad to hear it."

"Instead of focusing on the forbidden, what if I helped you find Mr. Right?"

Knight pulled out mugs from beside Lake's legs. "That sounds torturous."

Lake laughed. "Come on, it could be fun!"

Knight rose from a crouch, and a wash of air stirred over Lake. He settled the mugs on the counter beside Lake, then stepped in front of him.

Tightening everywhere, Lake blinked hard at the swift, powerful response.

"No more talk about matching me up with someone else, okay?"

Knight cupped his knees, hot palms and skating thumbs on his bare skin, and gently urged Lake's thighs apart.

Lake's breath hitched. "What are you—?"

Knight pulled out the cutlery drawer and drew out a couple of teaspoons.

Oh.

Lake clamped a hand over his nape. He suppressed a panicked chuckle. He didn't suppress the tickles Knight left behind on his knees—that sensitive skin on the inner side . . .

The scent of percolating coffee lured a bouncy Harry in jean shorts, an epically bright pineapple-print shirt, and matching socks.

"Coffee?" Knight offered.

Harry accepted a cup and downed it in three large gulps. "Sorry, got to run for the bus. Audition. Cashier man, three lines! Wish me luck."

The moment the front door shut, Lake snuck into the chaotic shambles of Harry's room.

"Lake?"

Lake jumped, swinging toward Knight who frowned at him from the doorway, cradling a mug of steaming coffee. "Shit, you surprised me."

"I wish I could say the same. Why are you sifting through Harry's things?"

"If you came to bring me sustenance, you can leave the coffee on the desk."

Knight sipped. "You can pour your own. Right now might be a good idea."

"Just a sec." Lake plucked through a mound of laundered but unfolded clothes.

"What are you doing?"

Lake draped a yellow and green smiley-face shirt over his shoulder. Where was the strawberry-print one? "You didn't see anything, Knight. Have we ever used our fireplace?"

"Our?"

Lake looked at him over his shoulder. "Rent. I should start paying you. We'll chat after you start the fire."

"What's gotten into you?"

"The same as every other day the last year. Nothing."

Regret immediately chased Lake's snarky reply.

Wooden floorboards groaned as Knight shifted in his peripheral vision, and the hairs on the back of Lake's neck prickled at the sudden thickening quiet.

Lake rifled through Harry's clothes with fervor. "Ah ha!" He pulled out the strawberry-print shirt. "He'll thank me one day."

"Leave it, Lake. Harry is cute enough without you changing his style."

"You think so?"

"Yes, and those shirts are part of his personality. He suits them."

Lake plucked the shirts off his shoulder, inspected them, and then Knight. "I want to help him make good impressions."

"He makes them. Especially since you've coaxed him out of his initial bashfulness."

"Knight!" Lake said, shocked.

"What?"

"That was a compliment. You never compliment me."

Knight laughed, and coffee splashed over the edge of his mug. He sipped. "You've a short memory."

"Being beautiful doesn't count. That's genetics. Nothing I've earned."

A soft smile pulled at Knight's lips and his eyes danced. He took a slow sip of his coffee. "Put those shirts down, and I'll tell you something else you'll like."

Lake dropped the shirts and marched to Knight, taking his spot against the doorframe. He folded his arms and waited.

Knight indulged in another sip, a playful smirk lighting his face. "I ran into Martin the other day."

"Where does this guy work? Harry ran into him too."

"A block from my office. We ducked into Tranquil for a coffee."

Lake nodded slowly. "Did you give him more advice on stock funds?"

"I gave him advice, but not on stocks."

Lake's stomach knotted. He wasn't liking this at all.

He stole Knight's coffee; Knight barely blinked.

"He told me he cares about Harry."

"So he should," Lake muttered into the mug. "They're cousins."

"They're more than that. Come on, Lake. You know Harry is in love with Martin."

Lake bristled. "I do not."

"Ridiculous. You figured it out at the barbecue."

Lake picked invisible lint from his shirt. "I mean, sure, Harry had a crush on Martin. But love? Neither of us knows that."

"You don't seem thrilled. I thought you were all about Harry and Philip finding romance."

"With *each other*."

Knight snorted. "That was never going to happen."

Knight had no idea. He wasn't in tune with Harry and Philip like Lake was. "What advice did you give lying Martin then?"

"Lying Martin?"

"He lied about being sick as an excuse not to come to our barbecue."

Knight's eyes shuttered. "Our?"

Lake glared over the mug, exasperated. "Martin or rent, which do you want to discuss?"

"You're right, he lied about being sick. He admitted as much to me over coffee. He was grappling with the magnitude of his feelings for Harry and needed the space. Seeing Harry again punched everything into perspective. Harry is the man he's in love with. He doesn't care that they're loosely related, and I supported him."

"Loosely?"

"Lake . . ."

"You don't make sense. You said you wouldn't get involved with the forbidden yourself, so why would you encourage Martin and Harry to?"

"They like each other, that's the difference."

"So if your crush liked you back, you'd go for it?"

Knight hesitated, and that said everything.

"You *would.*" Lake shook his head incredulously. "You said it'd be better if nothing happened."

"Maybe I'm over the concept of forbidden." Knight pushed off the doorway, his body crowding Lake. Every inch of skin pebbled with goosebumps. "Maybe I encouraged Martin, because I wanted to encourage myself."

"I don't believe it," Lake said, voice cracking. "You're too levelheaded to do anything off-limits."

Fingers drummed over the doorframe above his head and Knight leaned close. "It feels like you're baiting me, Emerett Lakewood."

His full name slid through Lake with an intimate shiver.

"Baiting! Ha! It's not like Paul's here for you to prove the point."

"*You're* here." Knight curled a gentle finger under Lake's chin and Lake met his intense gaze. "My son's best friend."

Shivers reigned.

Knight was determined to prove a point.

Their chests rose and fell, breaths mingling. Lake clutched the mug against his sternum.

The air thinned, yet Knight didn't move. His gaze dropped to Lake's lips and lingered.

His grip on the frame shifted and those beautiful brown eyes met Lake's again with a muted groan.

Lake squeezed the handle of the mug and whispered, "Far too level-headed."

Knight pressed a soft finger against his mouth, then traced the outline of Lake's lips.

Knight's mouth pinched together in a silent curse.

And then it happened.

Knight pressed against him, stomach against the coffee mug, leg nestled between his with tantalizing friction at his crotch.

One hand fell from the doorframe and cupped the crook between Lake's neck and shoulder; the other tightened at his waist. Knight's pinkie slipped under the hem of Lake's polo and Lake felt it like a plug to a socket.

He gasped, and Knight drank it in.

Shock rendered Lake motionless as Knight brushed the softest kiss from one corner of his mouth to the other.

Lake's breath hitched, lips parting, and Knight hummed, dipping to capture his bottom lip. Sensation surged through Lake; his knees buckled, and Knight braced him against the frame. A low, surprised sound vibrated out of Lake, and Knight drew back an inch. Their gazes held for an electrical second, and softly uttered words fanned over Lake's lip.

"Maybe we need to bury our fear of the forbidden."

"Maybe." Lake shook off those persistent shivers at his side, at his lips. "What were we talking about?"

"Rent. You want to move in permanently."

Surprised laughter bubbled out of him. God, he felt lightheaded. "*Martin.* Look, I'm guessing you told him to take Harry out for dinner? Maybe ask him to move back in?"

Knight's shrewd gaze latched on his suspiciously. "What do you know?"

"Martin asked Harry last night, and Harry let him down gently."

Knight's face crunched into confusion. "What?"

Lake repeated himself, and Knight's jaw twitched in indignation. "Why would he do that? Did he misunderstand?"

"He wasn't one-hundred percent sure of Martin's feelings, but he was sure of his own."

"What did you do, Emerett?"

This time Knight's emphasis on his first name did not feel good.

Lake lifted his chin. "He was hesitating. He said that probably wasn't a good sign."

"You persuaded him into letting him down."

"I told him he was the only one who could look into his heart."

"I know you. Your silence would have said a thousand other things." Knight strode toward the kitchen.

Lake followed with a miserable lump in his stomach, and a stubborn one in his throat.

"Jesus, Lake. You have no idea of your influence."

"Harry is a grown man—"

"Who wants you to like him."

Knight poured himself another coffee.

Lake couldn't stomach a drop more, but he refilled his mug anyway.

Knight cursed under his breath. "I warned you not to mess with people's love lives."

"He really likes Philip! Maybe turning Martin down was meant to be."

Knight set his coffee down, grabbed his phone from the

charger, and slipped it into his pocket. "I hoped you'd see it for yourself, but enough. Philip is not moon-eyed over Harry."

Fright prickled Lake. What did he mean? Surely not . . . no. Outrageous.

Knight didn't pay close attention like Lake did. Lake had seen Philip and Harry's spark. It was cheerful and sweet and worth pursuing.

"Where are you going?" Lake demanded.

Knight could barely look at him. "I need a walk. Don't touch any more of Harry's things."

"You're that mad at me?"

"I'm that frustrated."

Lake's stomach dove out of his feet. It took everything to hold his head high. "I only wanted him happy," he called after a retreating Knight.

The front door shut with typical Knightly restraint.

Lake sagged against the counter and tipped his coffee down the drain.

Knight was wrong.

Certainly about Philip, and tonight would prove it.

L ake sat cross-legged, surrounded by a moat of open books.

Knight returned after an hour's "walk" and strode directly to the back yard, not commenting on Lake's intensive study of Shakespeare, Bacon, Austen, and Christie.

Words blurred. He *was* sorry. But . . . he couldn't say it. Worse, he itched to prove he was right about Philip and Harry.

He *was* right, wasn't he?

He jerked his fingers from his mouth. He needed to stop tracing over the lingering weight of Knight's kiss.

The lure of the forbidden is what made it feel like he was falling from great cliffs, chasing gravity. Thrills unparalleled.

If this was what Harry felt for Martin . . .

Lake understood how tempting it was.

How easily one could confuse it with having *feelings*.

But there were no feelings between him and Knight. Absolutely none. Knight was Lake's biggest critic, and his kiss was merely an illustration of his refusal to be pegged as level-headed.

Being level-headed was one of Knight's best qualities. Lake gritted his teeth at Paul throwing Knight's good traits down the drain.

Love was stupid without someone impartial to guide it.

Lake vowed to forget Knight's moment of weakness, steer him toward available men, and never think of that kiss again.

Footsteps thumped down the hall and Harry emerged,

hugging a bucket of Ben & Jerry's. He grabbed two spoons, jumped over Lake's moat, and collapsed beside him.

Lake dug into some cookie dough. "Didn't go well?"

"My lines went fine, and my monologues were good. Until they asked for more."

Lake winced sympathetically. "You didn't have more?"

"Nope. I completely blanked." Harry sucked ice cream off his spoon, then waved the spoon at the books around them. "What's this?"

"The definition of pitiable."

Harry nodded compassionately and picked up *Mansfield Park*. "Ohhh, I love Austen. Well, okay, I've only seen the film adaptions. But I love imagining living in one of her worlds."

Lake shook his head, aghast. "With all those meddling mothers? Good thing you're spending the summer with me. Now, let's find you a perfect monologue."

"How will we do that?"

Lake held out his hand. "Pass me your phone."

"It's charging in the kitchen," Harry said around a mouthful of ice cream.

Lake pulled out his own phone and started swiping. "We need someone smart, who loves to read."

"Knightly?"

Lake paused, fingers on the screen. "No. *Philip*."

Lake: Help me choose a monologue for Harry?

Philip: What kind of monologue?

Lake: Something emotional. Heartfelt. Something that makes me catch my breath when Harry performs it.

Philip: Sounds like a fun afternoon.

Lake: Would you like to join us?

Philip replied swiftly, promising to be at their place within the hour. He also attached a monologue.

"Guess you should read it," Lake said, passing his phone to Harry.

Harry scrolled through and started trembling. "That's an interesting choice. Right?"

Lake scrutinized the text.

There. Proof. Impossible to get any clearer about how Philip felt about Harry. Though taking a love quote from *Romeo and Juliet* seemed a little inappropriate.

He was probably too excited to find something less tragic.

"Very interesting." Lake tiptoed out of the moat. Was that the lawnmower he heard? "We should choose an answering monologue to perform to Philip when he arrives."

"We should?" Harry and his pineapples scurried over to him.

Lake held back from suggesting he change. If only Knight were there to witness the feat. "We'll practice in the gazebo."

"It's not too much?"

"Much?"

"You know, grand-gesturey."

Lake scoffed. "Actors thrive on the dramatic."

"Ever thought about acting?"

Lake gave Harry a double-take. He waggled a finger, grinning, and scooped up a frightened Garfield en route to the gazebo. "You've been hanging around Knight too long."

He cuddled Garfield close, kissing her furry head.

"Holy crap," Harry murmured as they approached the gazebo. "Knightly's shirtless."

Lake pulled up from Garfield's ears.

He tried hard not to gawk at those muscles flexing under a sheen of sweat as Knight worked the mower . . .

Harry cocked his head. "He's hot."

Lake petted Garfield harder. "He's lucky. True attractiveness takes effort. It comes from the heart and the mind."

"Which would make Knight . . .?"

Dangerous.

Lake plunked himself and Garfield on a bench inside the gazebo. "Let's practice your monologue."

"We don't have one."

Lake fished for his phone and searched. Definitely had to be Shakespeare, to respond in the same language . . .

Not that.

Definitely not that.

What the hell did *that* even mean?

"Got it. I'm forwarding to you."

Harry's freckled cheeks bunched in a cheerful smile. "So sweet. I hope I can deliver the lines without blushing."

"Blush. Philip would like that."

"Speaking of blushing," Harry said curiously. "Who makes *you* stupid?"

Please. "No one."

"When we first met, I was sure you'd be in a relationship."

"Nope. No luck in that department. Probably never fall in love."

"Oh, you will," Harry said softly. "It'll sneak up on you and cause all kinds of trouble." He sighed.

Lake swallowed a longing lump in his throat, and watched Cameron blindly feeling for his poolside towel next door.

"What about him?"

"Cameron?"

"He's good looking and smart. Has his own YouTube channel. He said he'd let me know if they run auditions."

"Cameron isn't into me. Not the way he's into Jane Austen, his brother, and *Josh who graduated from Oxford.*"

Harry looked at him questioningly.

A cheeky wink. "Josh is a neighbor who didn't invite me to his upcoming party."

Harry bobbed his head. "Ah. You're holding a grudge."

"What gave me away?"

They laughed and returned to Harry's monologue and the task of perfecting his delivery. Lake concentrated hard.

So hard, there was no time for his gaze to stray across the freshly cut lawn to—

"I'm parched."

Harry ran off, and with the sudden stilling of the lawn-mower, Garfield trotted after him.

A shiver zipped over Lake. He felt Knight's attention on him. His frustration. His displeasure.

How long would he stay upset?

It burned in Lake's gut. He wanted things normal again.

Lake groaned, knowing he'd have to acknowledge Knight's concerns.

He found Knight half-naked in the shadowy shed, bent over the garden hose and sprinklers. The point at Lake's waist and the insides of his knees where Knight had touched him this morning pulsed. His mind turned to mush.

He breathed in deeply. Cut grass, honeysuckle, and *Knight*.

Sensing Lake, Knight straightened, but didn't turn around. "Lake."

Words fell from his lips unbidden. "My bounty is as boundless as the sea, my love as deep; the more I give to thee, the more I have, for both are infinite."

Knight whisked around, and Lake staggered back at the colliding currents, flustered. "The monologue Philip suggested for Harry. See, I was right. Philip does crush on him."

Not how he intended to start this conversation. For fuck's sake, what was wrong with him?

Shadows clouded Knight's expression. "O hell! To choose

love by another's eye." He leaned closer, stealing Lake's air. "In simpler English: poor Harry."

Disagreement and vexation thickened in the air between them, and Lake hated how he couldn't find an excuse for his provocative outburst. He was as upset with himself as Knight was.

Just too stubborn to voice it.

"Lake?" Harry called from the distance, splicing the tension.

Lake rocked back on his heels, shoving his hands into his pockets. "*Poor Harry* awaits."

He shot out the shed door, and Knight's deep sigh followed him.

Harry trundled toward him with a beaming Philip, who was dressed for church rather than an afternoon in the garden. An elegant shirt and black socks under black slacks. Though anything might look elegant next to the pineapples . . .

Philip embraced him with an excited squeeze and a croaky "Can't wait to hear this monologue" in his ear.

Lake drew back, smiling hard. "No point drawing out the suspense. Harry, let's do this."

Harry jumped to his spot on the gazebo. "Okay, but I only agreed to this because Lake has a flair for the dramatic."

Lake pulled Philip down on the bench next to him. "The bigger, the better."

Philip clapped, "Let's hear it, then."

Harry bowed his head and sucked in a deep breath. When he raised his head, Harry was gone, and Shakespeare's Demetrius stood before them. "To what, my love, shall I compare thine eyne?"

Under his breath, Philip mused, "Not my monologue then?"

"An answer to it."

Philip's eyes lit up and his cheeks flushed. All his attention honed in on Harry and his spectacular performance.

"Crystal is muddy. O, how ripe in show
　"Thy lips, those kissing cherries, tempting grow!
　"That pure congealed white, hight Taurus' snow,
　"Fanned with the eastern wind, turns to a crow
　"When thou hold'st up thy hand. Oh, let me kiss
　"This prince of pure white, this seal of bliss!"

Philip rubbed his knees nervously. "What an answer," he murmured.

Lake gave himself a metaphorical pat on the shoulder. "Note the tweak from 'princess' to 'prince' in the final line."

Philip's eyes lit up and his cheeks flushed. "For me?"

"Who else?"

Philip looked at Lake, astonished, touched, a little like he might burst out into a *yippee*.

When Harry bowed, Philip stood, clapping loudly.

"I messed up one line," Harry said regretfully, cheeks pinked.

"Sounded perfect to me. Would you do it again?"

"Again? Oh, uh, sure." Harry stretched, shaking himself once more into character.

"Are you okay, Lake?" Worry creased Philip's brow.

Lake blinked up at him. "Huh?"

Philip gestured to Lake's finger. "You keep touching your lips."

Lake jerked his hand to his side, then sat on it for good measure. "Just a little ticklish."

A sparkle hit Philip's eye and he resumed his seat, angling toward Lake. "I might have something for that."

Water sprayed over the back of their heads, and cold droplets glided under Lake's collar. Lake swung around.

Knight—who'd put on his shirt but left it unbuttoned—adjusted the sprinklers behind them. "Sorry."

He looked anything but.

Lake had left that shed too early. Too many frustrations festered between them. Three hours of Knight's unhappiness with him was agony. Lake couldn't take it anymore.

"Enjoy the monologue, guys. I'll be back."

Lake launched himself out of the gazebo, curled a hand around unsuspecting Knight's, and towed him into the house.

10

Taylor's bedroom had the best view of the backyard, so that's where Lake headed.

The second he stepped inside, awkwardness flooded him. He breathed in the familiar mustiness, looking from the foosball table to the massive oak bed where Lake had spent countless nights talking to Taylor about stupid frat boys. And lying assholes. And whether he'd ever find true love.

His fingers, clutching Knight's, pulsed wildly.

Knight removed his hand, clearing his throat. "Is there a reason we're in here?"

Lake fought the guilty rise and fall in his belly and sat on a bench by the large windows. "We're here to talk."

Knight quietly absorbed his son's room. "I see. This room gives you the necessary perspective."

The best perspective on Cameron's pool next door, and the gazebo. "It does."

Lake stared down at the lovebirds and sighed. Knight slipped beside him, a foot away. Buzzing energy stirred over his entire body.

Lake halted his fingers in their journey toward his mouth, and cleared his throat. They were there to overcome their disagreement. "I hate this awkwardness between us."

Without meeting his eye, Knight inclined his head. "I understand."

"You do?"

"I'll back off."

Lake should have been happy that Knight wanted to withdraw his criticism, but he rarely experienced it with anyone else. Even Taylor sugar-coated the truth.

Knight was superiorly, annoyingly honest with him.

And it was impossible to confess how much he liked it. "Back off, good. Good. Really good." He extended a hand. "Friends?"

Knight shook with a warm parting squeeze. "As you wish."

Tremendous pressure lifted off Lake, and he bubbled with laughter. "We agree to disagree regarding Philip and Harry?"

"We agree to disagree. But for the record, I'm right."

Lake slapped his arm. "That's not how it works—and you're totally not!"

Knight laughed. "I'm older and wiser, remember."

"Without the wrinkles to show for it!"

Their amusement faltered and Lake flushed, ears ringing. An uneven breath left him, and at Knight's gentle frown, Lake looked out the window. "Pass me Taylor's binoculars? On the bookshelf, next to the globe."

Seconds later something heavy landed in his open palm. Lake caught the book before it tumbled. *The Princess Bride.*

"If it's romance you want," Knight said. "Read this."

"It'll have to join my big, fat moat of books downstairs."

"It's not about how many you read, Lake. It's about how thoroughly you read them."

Lake hugged the book to his chest, smirking. "I'm spying on Harry and Philip now. Stay if you want, but no commentary."

"I'll return to the garden."

Lake shrugged. "I mean, a little commentary never hurt."

"Do you want me to stay, Lake?"

"Yes, please."

Knight scooped up Taylor's binoculars. "A *lot* of commentary."

He traded binoculars for the book and perched on the sill across from Lake.

The lovebirds stood together in the gazebo, soft golden light stretching over them like a fairytale. Philip looked toward Harry, and—smiled?

Lake side-eyed Knight, triumphant. Any moment Philip and Harry would kiss, if they hadn't already. All because of him.

"I don't like him," Knight said.

"Who?"

"Philip. He tries too hard and he clings to you."

"Clings to me?" Lake said, skeptical. "I think you mean Harry."

"Harry clings to you too. But not the same way."

Fright punched into him, but he shrugged it off. Harry and Philip stood so close—okay close-*ish*—and Harry was smiling. "You're seeing things."

"You're *not* seeing things."

"Philip and I are friends. We've volunteered together for months and he's never come on to me. Why would he now?"

"Maybe he was focused on someone else who didn't work out?"

Lake frowned. "Are you calling me his option B?"

Knight rolled his eyes. "Are you hearing my point?"

"You think Philip wants in my pants. I think you're wrong."

Knight leaned against the window frame and raised his palms. "It's just commentary."

"You should return to the garden."

Knight laughed, but it was Harry's sudden dash from the gazebo that stole Lake's attention. "What on earth?"

Lake raced downstairs, confusion hammering in his chest.

Harry burst into the kitchen, pale, Philip on his heels.

"I'm late," Harry said. "I forgot Grandma's birthday dinner. I need a present. I need to show up."

Lake sagged with relief against the oven. He thought maybe Philip had told Harry he wasn't interested in him, and Harry was heartbroken. But that was Knight getting into his head.

Harry was fine.

Late, and reliant on the bus system. But fine.

"Philip," Lake said, thinking quickly, "you live close to Harry's grandma, would you take him? Maybe drop in at a store on the way?"

"I wanted to spend more time here."

A tendril of alarm made Lake's belly sick, and he met Philip's eyes.

Philip waved away his complaint. "Of course I'll take Harry. I'd love to."

Lake let out a relieved breath. Philip had been disappointed his time with Harry had to end. That's all.

Shoes and crocodile-print shoes were donned, and Philip and Harry shrank down the path towards Philip's car.

Lake shut the door and sagged against it.

He must be imagining Philip's disappointment as he waved goodbye, and that offer to drive back again after . . .

The man was lonely. That was all.

Knight found him at the door. "Sprinkler's on a timer, I'm ready to eat." He gave Lake a double take. "Are you okay?"

"I need to flip my mattress."

Knight stopped stuffing his feet into a pair of brown sneakers. "What?"

"Gonna flip it real hard."

"Are we talking about actual mattresses?"

"I could flip yours, too."

"Okay, you really need to explain."

No way would he let Knight know there might be a teeny, *tiny* possibility he'd read Philip better. "I need to get my mind off things."

"And flipping mattresses helps?"

"It's also really good for the mattress."

Knight smiled grimly. "Get your shoes on. We're doing dinner."

11

They'd barely reached the tree-lined street when Cameron popped out from his car, waving.

Such a gorgeous man—a striking face, under the glasses. Pity his clothes were two sizes too big and cinched at the waist with a belt.

Clueless to the power of his killer dimpled smile.

Lake halted, arm brushing and lingering against Knight's, and prepared for an update on Cameron's LGBTQ+ period-drama YouTube channel. How he, his brother, and his crew were Live Streaming Austen monologues to grow their audience, how he had hired script writers and directors to adapt short classics into film. How they were running the operation from a friend's basement—

"Exciting news!"

"Exciting?" Lake said skeptically, earning a chastising glance from Knight.

Cameron nodded eagerly. "You know the queer Ask Adam advice column?" Okay, maybe Lake was listening. "The magazine's gone under—"

"Ask Adam's gone under?" Lake blurted. He loved that column.

"That's not the exciting part. The exciting part is they contacted me to see if I was interested in buying the rights to the concept for my channel."

Lake needed a moment to digest the speedily said words. "No more *My Bisexual Crush Dated My Sister and Now Wants to Date Me* commotions?"

Knight side-eyed him. "You were into them?"

"So dramatic," Lake said, because it said everything.

A low hum. "So forbidden."

The word dove through Lake, surfacing in rings of shivers at his hip, his knees, his crotch. His breath snagged and he was glad Cameron swiftly continued, "That's what I'm saying. My channel can adapt it! We'll redirect letters to us and Ask Adam—or rather *Ask Austen* —could deliver live responses based on quotes from Austen's works."

"Uh." The friction between their upper arms intensified, and Lake inched away. "That's such an opportunity. Really cool."

"Hey, did you ever get an invite to Josh's party?" Cameron always knew what to say.

Lake jerked a finger toward Knight from a safe distance, earning a raised brow. "Knight's taking me along."

"Oh," Cameron said, "Josh probably forgot to tell you about it."

Lake wasn't sure which was worse, being uninvited because he was a little too memorable, or overlooked because he was not memorable enough.

"He's too nice to do it on purpose," Cameron continued. "He's staying with his parents all summer. I'm sure you'll be friends by the end of it."

Wonderful. "Oh, shit. Josh from *Oxford*." Two pairs of baffled eyes landed on Lake as he smacked his forehead. "I forgot to text West."

Cameron brightened. "You mean Taylor's old best friend? He's around? He went off the radar."

"I thought you'd had a close history together?"

"Not much. West and Taylor went to a different high school, they barely came around. West headed to London for the big overseas experience, and when Josh got into Oxford for post-grad, I asked Taylor for West's number so Josh had another Kiwi contact over there. That's the extent of it."

Knight's frown deepened. "You're in touch with West?"

"I should have been!" Lake pulled out his phone out and finger-punched a message. "I promised Taylor I'd invite him to the party—by the way, what are we doing for Taylor and Amy's arrival?"

"Preparing their home. Making them dinner."

"Okay, sure—of course—but later that weekend?"

"What about another barbecue?"

Lake nodded. "With Karaoke this time, and someone else manning the grill."

"Is that an offer?"

"It is a nice grill, but you probably don't want just anyone touching it."

Knight snorted. "Good thing you're not *just anyone*."

Lake scowl-groaned. "Fine, I'll man the grill."

"I'll help," Cameron offered. "Another thing. We need to rebrand our channel, and I wanted to ask—"

"Oh damn," Lake said, taking Knight by the elbow and ushering him toward the car. "My appointment's in fifteen minutes. We've got to go, sorry."

As soon as the doors slammed shut, Knight gave him a silent reprimand.

Lake snapped his seatbelt in. "I know, I know. But he has a dream. He's actually making it happen. And the worst part? He's like you."

"How is being like me a worst part?"

"If there's a checklist, he's checking things off it."

Knight started the engine and looked at him, bewildered. "That's a bad thing?"

"A very *good* thing." He was happy for Cameron. Should support him more, but—"I'm jealous."

Knight hummed in agreement.

Lake folded his arms tightly against the uncomfortable truth. The fact was, everyone around him had veered into better jobs and found loving partners, while Lake didn't have a goal in his professional life, and in his personal . . . something was definitely missing.

Knight eyed him and chuckled. "You could always make a list of your own."

"I have a list. I just don't have someone to complete it for me."

Knight's hand shot off the gearstick and clasped his shoulder. "If you need help, Lake, you can always ask."

The pressure at his shoulder was comforting, and the accidental drift of Knight's finger over the base of his throat . . .

He raked a hand through his hair. "How do you feel about Chinese?"

Twenty-five minutes later, following Lake's instructions, they parked in the secluded lot of Lakewood Bourbon Distillery, boxed takeout heating their already warm laps.

They slurped delicious hot noodles. Lake dove his chopsticks into Knight's box for a wonton and Knight returned the favor, pinching a battered piece of sweet-and-sour chicken.

The brick facade glowed in the last stretches of light.

"How often do you come here?" Knight's question was quiet. So was the drawn beat after.

Lake pinched more noodles, then dropped them back into the box. "Couple of times a week, after work."

"Want to talk about it?"

Lake shook his head.

"Does Taylor know about this?"

"Coming here? No. That I take every opportunity to pity myself? Yes."

Knight didn't laugh. "He'd be there for you."

Lake swallowed. "I know. I should. It's just . . . there's no big story. He died. I'm sad. I don't know what else I'd say."

Knight cupped the back of Lake's hand and squeezed, and Lake closed his eyes at the comfort rolling through him. "Whenever you want to talk about it, Lake. Taylor's there for you, and so am I."

Lake blinked back tears and his throat tightened. He nodded, then reached over and swapped their takeout boxes. "Yours tastes better."

"Every time," Knight said.

When they'd finished their food and bottled water, Knight bagged the boxes and settled them behind Lake's seat. His breezy, fresh scent washed over Lake and he breathed it in.

"Want to go someplace?" Knight asked, one hand drifting lazily over the steering wheel. "We could grab a drink."

"Nah, I'm good."

"As much as I am here for you while you stare at your distillery all evening . . ."

Knight's gentle expression almost stole Lake's voice. "Less pathetic?"

Eyes twinkled. "Well . . ."

Lake bubbled with a laugh. Knight always had a way of eliciting one. "I might manage a drink after all."

"Good."

"We can talk about rent. And . . ."

"And, what?"

Lake took a deep breath. "Maybeyoucanhelpmesellmy-cottage?"

12

Lake begged Knight to wait until nine before heading to Josh's party. Not seven on-the-dot. No way could Lake seem desperate.

He paced the gazebo, peering down the line of backyards, scrutinizing Josh's. He could hear music, faintly. Was it busy enough yet?

From the bench, Knight looked up from his Kindle. "Don't worry. *Josh* won't think you're desperate."

"I'm not—fine, let's go."

On their way through the house, Lake knocked at Harry's door, opened, and winced. Poor Harry was bunched up in his bed with a stuffy red nose, used tissues carpeting his blankets.

"'Ake." Harry tried to smile, and it hurt to look at it.

"If you need anything, we're three houses down—"

Harry blew his nose, the sound trumpeting around them.

"—and it might be better if you stick to texting."

"I wish I could come. Tell Philip I'm sorry?"

"Sure, I'll—Philip will be there?"

He whipped his head toward Knight but he'd walked ahead, his flexing calves turning into the kitchen.

Lake glared toward Harry—the world—"Did *everyone* get an invite except me?"

Harry's voice crackled. "Philip went to high school with Josh."

"He did?"

"He told me on the way to Grandma's. He wondered if he should tell you he'd be there or keep it a surprise."

Why would he want to keep it a surprise?

Hairs at Lake's nape prickled, and he rocked back on his heels. Projecting unlikely *what ifs* into the universe was making him antsy. Philip expected *Harry* to meet him at Josh's. He'd shared parts of his childhood history with *Harry*.

Lake was fretting over nothing.

"It was so nice of him to take me there last weekend. He even bought me a Coke when we stopped for gas."

See, nothing.

"I'll tell him you're sorry you couldn't come. Should I send him here?"

"Not looking like this." Harry sighed, and then coughed into the crook of his arm. "Plus, I've taken something to knock me out."

Lake wished him goodnight and found Knight waiting at the front door. The corrugated brown gift box under his arm contained a bottle of Lakewood Bourbon, a gift from the both of them that Lake had picked. Totally without ulterior motives . . .

Knight had eyed it earlier—even withheld any criticism. Told Lake to do what he felt was right.

Which—no, it was a fine gift. It *was*.

Porch light glowed warmly over Knight and his nice sneakers, pressed navy shorts, tight white T-shirt under that soft-looking unbuttoned shirt. He looked crisp and fresh, with a pleasant hint of aftershave that reminded Lake how close they stood. Lake's throat tightened, along with his nipples, which he hoped didn't show through his thin green T-shirt.

Instinctively, he reached out and touched Knight's shirt—just as soft as he imagined. His grin felt lopsided. "Earthy tones have never looked better. Really complements your eyes."

Knight returned the slow-sweeping favor, and when their eyes met, nodded. "You work your colors, too."

He turned on his heel and kicked toward the street.

Lake smirked, and chased after him. "Are you admitting to making them stand out on purpose? Why, Knight. I never took you for vain."

A tight look. "By now you should know I'm full of vices."

"And sixteen virtues. Amending that to seventeen, since you spent most of the day fixing my cottage."

Knight waved the compliment away. "Just a few repairs that'll help it sell."

"A few?" Lake ticked off his fingers. "You replaced the broken towel rack, exchanged the sink and the master bedroom door handle—oh, and tiled the shower."

Shirtless.

But Lake wasn't replaying that in his mind or anything.

"Tomorrow we'll replace those dated light fixtures with something modern." Knight seemed to be mentally checking off boxes. "The house is nicely decluttered, except for your room." A couple of quiet beats passed. "You could move your things here?"

Lake cast his relief to the sun-setting pink above them. "God, I love you. Yes to everything."

Knight's step slipped.

Stupid gravel from the neighbor's driveway. Lake kicked it off the sidewalk and continued discussing the logistics of the next day, including breakfast. How could he ever repay Knight for being there? For that sympathetic, compassionate hug he'd given him on his brick path to bolster his confidence before heading into the Lakewood family home.

Knight frowned gently at the bourbon. Shit. The bourbon. Had Lake overdone the passive-aggressiveness? It's not like he enjoyed the thought of Josh forced to remember him whenever he drank from it . . .

Who was he kidding?

Lake was a terrible person. He should never have agreed to Knight censoring his criticism. He needed Knight telling him he was overstepping. Telling him that making a point was really a mimed bitch-slap.

Oh God, was it too late to change the gift?

They stepped over chalk arrows to the side of Josh's place. Music and chatter grew louder, somewhat buffered by a large gate with popped balloons. Cold, thick shadows fell from the stone house. Knight halted.

Lake twisted and leaned against the gate, not at all glancing over Knight's form, or feeling the block of heat of his broader body.

Lake swallowed, gaze straying to his immature boxed gift. "Knightly?"

"Emerett?"

"Remember when I agreed you should back off?"

"Vividly."

He gave in to a ridiculous urge to laugh, and shoved a hand through his hair. "Maybe a *little* less?"

Dark eyes snapped to his, and a tingling shiver threaded through Lake, from his scalp, down his spine, to his calves—his crotch, too. Definitely there.

The gate yanked open, and Lake lost his balance, falling backward. A wiry arm caught him at the elbow and hip, nails digging for purchase.

Lake cried out, "So sorry—"

"There you are."

He jolted upright.

Philip beamed at him, gaze bright. Possibly inebriated. He clapped. "Serendipitous. I was about to come get you myself."

A scoffing chuckle came from behind him. Lake scowled. No, he hadn't forgotten Knight's thoughts on Philip.

Or how desperately he needed Knight to be wrong.

Lake straightened his shirt, smiling. Friendly but not so friendly that it gave Philip the wrong idea. "Harry's sorry he can't come tonight."

Philip frowned in commiseration, but not long enough.

Knight was far too quiet, no doubt waiting for the moment to say "I told you so."

Knight could *not* be right about this. He was misreading the signs, and he'd damn well gotten into Lake's head.

Lake continued hurriedly, "He's really sick."

"Yeah, he texted me. Poor guy. He seemed excited for tonight." Philip's smile grew and he winked. "Guess we'll have to have more fun on his behalf."

Not quite the reaction Lake had expected. On the other hand, the two had been texting, so Philip already had time to process his disappointment.

Yes, that.

Lake quickened his step down the side of the house.

Josh's party was held in his foster parents' large backyard. At least fifty people were peppered in clusters.

Lounging against a lamppost next to the drinks station, laughing with his parents, was the man of the hour. Josh. Maori, sexy, and energetic. He hugged his mum and kissed her cheek.

A woman wearing a glittery top shrieked Philip's name. Philip blinked, confused, then roared back in recognition.

"Did you just arrive?"

"No, a bunch of us are in the back of the greenhouse."

She—*Connie*—dragged him toward the path. Some guy called Trey just *had* to see him again.

"Lake," Philip called over his shoulder, "did you want to come?"

Knight's breath tickled at the back of his ear, like he might be shaking his head while laughing.

"Go ahead," Lake said, slapping on a smile. "Gotta say hello to Josh."

"Okay, I won't be long."

"Take your time." *Please*.

Josh spotted them and beamed. He hugged Knight, and Knight murmured something that made Josh laugh.

Josh turned to Lake and hauled him into a hug. "Kia ora, man! Kei te pēhea?"

Lake dredged his memory for an appropriate te reo Māori response. "Kei te pai." Great. Primary school level skills.

Josh just smiled. His curly blue hair now had shaven zigzags on one side. "I'm glad you came! I didn't have your number."

Oh.

Lake had gotten a new number six months ago when his phone got stolen.

Crap.

"I asked Taylor for it, but all I got back was pictures of him and Amy in Madrid."

Lake would have a few words with Taylor later.

"And I should've asked Knight, but I got busy. Forgot . . ."

Understandable. Lake shrugged, casual like. "I mean, I figured it wouldn't have been a nefarious reason."

Knight chortled and coughed into his fist. "We're sorry you couldn't make it to the wedding."

Lake agreed. "It was wonderful, from their heart-melting vows to the mouth-watering crostini."

That last bit earned him a quiet shake of Knight's head.

"Crostini? Tell me more." Josh laughed and listened attentively. Like *really* attentively.

Was he checking Knight out?

Knight seemed to catch the glance too. He raised their gift. "Yes, for you."

Oh crap, the gift.

Maybe Josh would be touched Lake had given him such a personal gift.

What was he thinking? Josh knew Lake enough to know what he meant by the gift.

"So, Oxford graduate," Lake blurted, drawing Josh's attention away from the box. Maybe he wouldn't open it until later? Never? "What's next?"

Josh laughed. "Everyone's favorite question."

He opened the box—Lake cringed—and pulled out a bottle of zinfandel.

Knight watched every emotion—regret, embarrassment, hope—pass over Lake's face. How well Knight knew him. How very perceptive. And maddening.

But mostly, how very relieving.

In a wash of men's cologne, Josh hugged and thanked them, then moved the wine to a gift shelf.

Lake sidled closer to Knight, until their elbows knocked. "I could mostly kinda kiss you right now."

"I would mostly kinda not stop you."

Lake laughed, nervously. Knight was only joking, but Lake kind of, maybe, *really* wanted to. Lake stared at those gently smiling lips, shivering at the stir of Knight's hitching breath.

"Philip says you and he are volunteering together?" Josh's sudden reappearance was disorienting.

"Um, yeah."

"He'll be happy to see you. He's around here somewhere." Josh scoped the lawn. "Excuse me, Cameron's waving me over . . . enjoy yourselves."

Josh hiked off.

"I thought you'd be happy Philip's here?"

Lake shoved his hands into his pockets. "Sure I am. It's a shame Harry's sick. Philip seemed devastated when I told him."

"Was that devastated?"

Lake playfully shoved Knight toward the table. "Let's get drinks."

Knight rocked back with it, laughing. "I'm feeling quite good without the alcohol."

Lake, too. The lighthearted familiar cheek was comforting. His fingers splayed over Knight's T-shirt, and the open shirt fell softly over his knuckles. Knight's gaze twinkled, and woozy butterflies flapped around in Lake's stomach.

"Oh look, Philip's finished in the greenhouse. Perhaps I need a drink after all."

Knight pivoted to the buffet of beverages; Lake desperately dashed for a large lemon bush.

He peered through the leaves at Philip jouncing down the glasshouse steps.

Knight pivoted toward the space Lake had been and halted, perplexed.

In five eager strides, Philip joined him. "Do you know where Lake is?"

"I wish I could say I do."

"Oh, right. If you see him, point him my way or tell him to text me."

Philip strode off, circling around the other pockets of people, neck stretched, searching for Lake.

A shadow fell over his side and Lake pulled back from the bushes.

Knight planted his hands on his hips. Lake gulped and plucked a lemon. "I wanted a little zest in my drink."

Knight's eyes narrowed. "Philip is looking for you."

"Oh, is he?"

Knight cast him a *good try* look, and Lake didn't like the implications.

Cavalierly, he threw the lemon and caught it again. "He probably wants to know if he should surprise Harry with a visit."

"Is that right?"

"But poor Harry will be asleep."

"You should tell Philip then."

Lake swallowed. "But he'll be gutted . . ."

"Is there another reason you don't want to talk to him?"

Lake forced a laugh of denial. "I'm looking forward to talking to him. We'll spend the evening talking about his heart-eyes for Harry."

Knight folded his arms. "Go on then."

Wise guy. Bastard.

Gripping his lemon, he reluctantly chased after Philip.

"Philip." He tapped Philip on the shoulder, but he was already whirling around.

"I was looking for you!"

Lake smiled weakly. "Yay, me too. Why didn't you tell me you knew a guy who lived on this street?"

Philip laughed cheerily. "It did surprise you then. Excellent. I mean, I mentioned knowing someone on this street, but it worked well that you didn't put two and two together."

"You mentioned knowing someone?"

"The first time I came over."

Lake rubbed his thumb over the lemon. "Huh. I don't remember."

Philip looked disappointed. "You might have been giggling at something Taylor sent you."

"Oh. Right. I should pay better attention."

That put the grin back on Philip's face. "You're forgiven. In this case it worked out. The idea came when Harry let on you love grand gestures. I thought the surprise would be fun."

"Fun. Hmm,"—a nervous laugh tittered out of Lake —"definitely surprised me."

Philip beamed, gesturing a few feet to their side. "The loveseat is free, shall we—"

"I don't have a drink!" Lake blurted. Philip startled, and Lake felt ridiculous. "I mean, you sit. I'll grab us some."

"Or I could get them?"

Lake took him by the arm as platonically as he could, and

steered him to the seat. "Hold this." He slapped the lemon into Philip's hand.

Philip's face brightened tenfold. "You're giving me your lemon?"

"Have at it. Suck it dry."

Philip giggled with a waggle of his brows. "I like being told what to do."

Lake whirled away, stomach churning like it might eat him from the inside out.

Philip was tipsy; his sense of humor had degraded a bit. If Harry were here, he'd be throwing one-liners at him.

Lake found Knight at the drinks station, engaged in conversation with Josh's parents. It was strange thinking Knight had raised kids at the same time on the same street, undergoing the same parental woes. Knight looked nothing like Josh's parents, although having your kid in your senior year of high school definitely made one younger than most other parents.

Knight's senior-year girlfriend had wanted to adopt out, and Knight—against the wishes of his family—kept Taylor himself. The night Taylor had told him that story, Lake had lain in Taylor's bed, aware that the dry-witted, decidedly funny hero who'd strapped Taylor to his chest while he made pizza deliveries, done his business degree long distance, and clawed together a life for himself and his boy was sleeping a few rooms down. Lake remembered asking Taylor when his dad learned he was bisexual. Taylor had scoffed. Said it was a miracle he was born, because his dad had never noticed another woman since.

"Hello to Lake?" A hand waved in front of his face. Sweet-dimpled Cameron was actually wearing jeans that fit tonight.

"Cameron, hi. Thank God. I need a favor. Would you sit next to Philip on the loveseat for however long you can keep him there?"

"Why don't you want to sit there?"

"Long story, in which I hope I'm very wrong. Anyway, I'll come back with drinks. Free your seat under no circumstances."

Cameron obliged, and Lake mixed orange juice with a splash of Coke which he would tell Philip was a tequila sunrise.

Knight caught his eye over Josh's mum's shoulder, and Lake raised his cups and winked. All good.

Nothing to worry about in the slightest . . .

13

Cameron kept his seat for over an hour. An impressive effort.

Cameron and Philip even bonded over Trey, who Cameron had recently hired to edit segments before they aired.

"He's diligent in his job," Cameron said, always seeing the good in everyone. Cameron turned to Lake. "Have you ever thought about working with—"

Philip dropped the lemon he'd been fondling and chased it with such vigor that the loveseat swung back and upended Cameron on the grass.

"So sorry, my bad," Philip said, clutching his lemon triumphantly.

Lake offered Cameron a hand up. Cameron frowned, mirroring Lake's thoughts exactly. Philip and alcohol clearly didn't mix. He'd feel embarrassed by his behavior in the morning.

Philip caught Lake's eye and deigned to wink.

Very, very embarrassed.

Lake furtively checked Knight hadn't seen it. He was pre-occupied with Josh's friends at the greenhouse. Thank God.

As if he felt Lake's stare across the yard, Knight looked over. Their gazes met for an oddly intense moment, rendering Lake more aware of himself—from the way he dug his shoes into the lawn to the bits of loose thread that he played with in his pockets.

Knight excused himself from the crowd, and each step closer had Lake's pulse jumping.

He wanted Knight and his solid presence next to him. On the other hand, Knight could *not* witness this . . . whatever it was.

Philip didn't know what he was doing.

In the last few steps, Knight's mouth tipped upwards and an eyebrow quivered higher than the other. Light filtering through the bush speckled Knight's cheeks and hair, adding to the twinkle in his eye. Carefully controlled humor cloaked him like a nimbus. Contagious.

It took considerable effort to not to break out into a grin.

"Oh, Knight," Lake said, feigning concern. "You look exhausted. Are you heading home?"

"Exhausted?"

"It's been a really long day," Lake hurriedly explained to Cameron, who stood awkwardly near the loveseat. Philip had propped himself up on an elbow and was leering at him.

Lake steered Knight away by the elbow. "A good sleep will help."

Cameron nodded like it was a sensible decision, and Philip agreed. Rudely. "It's almost eleven, and you're no spring chicken."

Annoyance creased the corner of Knight's lips, but he held it in. He leaned in and spoke low in Lake's ear, the words a ticklish puff in his hair. "Why are you angling for me to leave?"

"Will you?" Lake asked hopefully under his breath.

"Not unless you explain or—"

"Or?"

"Leave with me."

Definitely that one.

"Actually," Lake announced, smiling in Cameron and Philip's direction. "I'm done with a big crowd too."

Philip swung his legs off the loveseat. "You want to be someplace quiet? Private?"

"My bed." Lake continued steering Knight away. "Later."

"Later," Philip replied, waving, a drunken smirk stretched across his face.

Lake didn't let go of Knight's elbow until they'd left Josh's and were, well, home.

They traipsed up the groaning stairs, and a yawn escaped Lake. "I'm gonna hit the sack."

He strode into his bathroom and stripped off his jeans and T-shirt, but he couldn't summon the energy for a shower. He'd do it in the morning.

A knock came at the door. "Is the bathroom free?"

Lake stuffed his clothes into the hamper and opened the door to Knight's room. Knight rocked on his heels at the sudden puff of air and Lake—practically naked—before him. "You could have said it was occupied."

Knight's gaze did not stray any lower than Lake's eyes, and disappointment wormed low in Lake's gut. Not that he expected Knight would *want* to look at him—why would he? He was in love with Paul and probably saw Lake as a miscreant accidental son.

Knight's lack of interest should have stopped Lake from checking him out, but He. Couldn't. Help. Himself.

"Just need to brush my teeth," Lake murmured.

Knight cleared his throat. "Me too. I can wait."

"Don't be ridiculous," Lake said, top of his ass bashing into the sink. "We can do it together. I mean, at the same time. Where are your pajamas?"

"Pajamas?"

"Your two-piece flannel suit. The one that buttons to the throat."

"I don't own such a thing."

"You should."

Knight's eyes sparkled like they held a secret. "Why should I wear pajamas?"

"Because you're . . ." Lake waved vaguely in Knight's direction.

"I'm . . .?"

"A dad. You shouldn't be sleeping in only a pair of tighty-whities. At the very least wear socks."

"Socks."

"Yes, because there's something intimate about not wearing socks in bed. All those nerve-endings sliding through soft cotton sheets . . ."

Knight beheld Lake with patient bemusement. "Dads aren't allowed intimacy?"

"No! Yes. No, that's not what I meant." Could Lake mess this up any more? "Yes, of course dads can be intimate." He felt stupidly aware of the goose bumps covering his body. "It's just . . . Know what? Let's just brush our teeth."

Lake paid more attention to dental hygiene than he ever had. Each tooth held his full attention. The mirror spitting back their mostly naked bodies crammed close? Not even a glance.

A loud *ping* sounded from Lake's room, followed by another sharp *ping* on glass. What the hell?

Lake yanked open his window and peeked out in time for a stone to flick his nose. Lake blinked through the sting. Philip spoke from below. "Oopsies."

"What are you doing?" Lake hissed.

Philip grabbed hold of the trellis, gave it a testing shake, and heaved himself up. "The ultimate grand gesture."

Lake's stomach sickened with realization. He attempted to stay calm, but with each foothold and upward purchase on the trellis, he seized with discomfort.

Not to mention the prickly awareness of Knight watching from the bathroom.

"You're drunk, Philip. You mean to do this for Harry."

"Harry?" Philip scoffed. "Why would I climb a trellis to Harry's room, besides the fact he's on the ground floor."

"Because you like him. Like-like him."

"I don't like-like him, I like-like *you*."

Lake jerked back when Philip reached the top.

"No, you don't like me. This is the alcohol talking."

"I had a few, so I could finally get the guts to express myself. I'm tipsy, not drunk."

"But—but Harry! You've spent the last weeks flirting with him!"

"You're joking," Philip cried. "Not once have I thought of him as anything other than your friend."

"But you gushed over his pictures! You sent him that subtext-rich monologue."

"I gushed over pictures *you* took. I sent *you* the monologue —to inspire feelings in *you*."

Lake's stomach dropped to his knees. He'd never felt so sick. Realizing he was wrong, that all Knight's concern had been warranted . . .

God, it was hard to breathe.

Philip hefted himself a foot higher, chest at the windowsill now. "I promise you, I've never wanted Harry. I was sure you were giving me signals."

"Signals?" Lake fervently shook his head. "There were no signals."

"You invited me to dinner after work. You chose that responding monologue."

"Outrageous. Well, technically you're right, but it was on Harry's behalf."

Philip reached into his shirt and pulled out a lemon. "You gave me this."

Lake blinked. "So?"

"It's your lemon."

Where was this going? "Yes?"

Philip held it up triumphantly and waggled his brows. "The catholic symbol for love and fidelity. You gave me your lemon. You wanted me to suck it dry."

Philip gave it an obscene squeeze.

Lake gaped. Unpleasant, awkward sensations overwhelmed him. He hated how sexual Philip made it all sound. Hated that Knight must have heard it.

"I-I didn't say I wanted you to suck it dry. I mean, I did, but I'm not Catholic. Neither are you."

"I read it somewhere, and the way you insisted on me having it . . ." Philip frowned. "You've eyed me, you've winked at me, you've texted me every other day. You practically told me you wanted to be alone with me. I think you *do* like me but you're freaking out."

Speechless. Lake was speechless.

Philip started climbing over the sill. "Let's try it. Let's fool around and see if it's good."

That bolted Lake into action—into leaping backwards. "No! I'm sorry if I looked at you the wrong way. Very sorry for sending unintentional messages. But I was trying to set you up with Harry."

"You're kidding," Philip said tightly.

Lake shook his head. "I'm not."

Philip let out an angry, hurt huff. "Harry is nice, in a buffoonish kind of way. But he's not a nine, like you and me."

Philip's gaze darkened with resentment as he clambered over the sill. He fell forward; Lake reached to steady him, only to be shaken off.

In mutual mortification, he watched as Philip let himself out of the bedroom and stomped down the stairs.

The front door slammed, and Lake winced.

The absurd moment played painfully over in his head as he turned away from the door to Knight, leaning cross-armed against the bathroom counter. Profound embarrassment zigzagged through Lake, making it impossible to meet his eyes.

He tried to find his voice, but only a croak came out.

That was it. Lake was *done*.

He flung himself across his bed.

14

The pillow scratched Lake's cheek where he buried his head, miserable.

He couldn't decide what felt worse—his embarrassment, or his disappointment. Believing he was uniting two socially awkward guys had given him ridiculous pleasure.

Harry would be gutted.

That was the worst part. Way worse than how utterly humiliated *he* was. He'd screwed with Harry's feelings. Given him false expectations; told him Philip was crushing on him.

God, he had screwed up so bad.

Breezes gushed over his bare skin, a cool reminder of the embarrassing events at the window. He shuddered.

Wood squealed—the sound of the window being shut—and Lake cringed at Knight's heavy footsteps moving toward the bed. He couldn't handle Knight's criticism tonight, even if he had asked Knight to hold back less.

"Here to tell me I told you so?" Sheets muffled his words, and the mattress dipped at his side. Knight sat back against the headboard, legs stretched along Lake's side, close to his arm.

"No." Fingers fluttered over Lake's hair. Soft, gentle touches that felt too forgiving. Nothing he deserved. But Lake couldn't bring himself to tell Knight to stop.

He turned his head toward—the curve of Knight's ass, squashing his pillow. He rolled onto his side. A peach moonlight glow stretched from the bathroom into his darker room.

Knight looked down at him fondly, like he genuinely was

on Lake's side and always would be—even if they disagreed—and Lake's emotions seeped to the surface.

"How could I have been so wrong? He wasn't interested in Harry at all." Lake had really, *truly* thought . . . "I was so bent on them getting together, I searched for it. Saw romance where there was none." He sighed, needing Knight to see he had genuinely misunderstood. "Philip had been so excited about Harry's pictures. And the monologue—I should have known it would end badly."

Knight had removed his fingers and they rested above Lake's head, brushing the ends of his hair. Lake wanted more affectionate petting, but he totally didn't deserve it.

Knight read him, and curled his fingers through Lake's hair to his scalp. "You meant well."

Lake held back from sighing at how good it felt. "Thinking about Philip is making me flinch, Knight. I thought he was a nice guy."

"He was nice to *you*. Exceptionally nice."

"God, you were right all along yet I refused to believe you. Even had the delightful urge to prove you wrong."

"Delightful urge?"

"You know, like a constant need for you to see me doing something right. Or, at least, something not wrong."

Knight breathed out heavily, long and slow, and his fingers rested against Lake's hairline, one finger sliding over his temple.

"I was wrong, though. Very wrong. Philip wasn't even that nice. How dare he talk about Harry like that? And wanting me only because I'm a nine . . ."

Guilt and disappointment flooded him, and his throat tightened. "Would you, like, scooch down so I can see your face better?"

Knight shuffled lengthwise next to Lake. He tucked the pillow under his head so nothing buffered their view. Knight's expression seemed cautious and pensive, and Lake yearned to read Knight as well as Knight read him. Closeness shivered through him, and Lake snuggled an inch nearer to the promise of all that warmth and comfort. He inhaled the fresh scent of him and let it out, miserably. "Why can't I be more like you? Ceaselessly sensible and smart."

A soft laugh puttered against Lake's jaw. "I'm not always sensible."

It took all of Lake's control not to stare at Knight's lips. "You're ninety percent sense, and that's eight-five percent more than me."

"Ninety is far too generous. I had a kid in my senior year of high school, remember?"

Lake studied Knight's lips. "It's hard to imagine you so horny you'd forget a condom."

"It broke."

Lake groaned. "That doesn't make you less sensible, just less lucky."

"I should have checked the use-by date."

Of course Knight would boil it down to that. "Aren't we lucky we have PrEP now?"

"Yes, well. I still carry a condom. I won't stop using one unless I'm in a long-term, trusting relationship."

"Fair. Do you ever still find women attractive?"

"We seem to have veered off topic."

Lake threw a hand over his face, groaning. "You're right. I'm sorry. I'll go back to dwelling on my failures."

Gently, Knight plucked Lake's hand off his face and pinned his fingers to the mattress. Softly, though. He could absolutely pull free, if he wanted to.

He didn't want to.

"No, I—no. Beth was the first person I told that I was into men, and somehow we agreed that we should at least try, to make sure. We were young. And superiorly stupid."

"Not tonight, because I have to face my own shittiness, but I'd like to hear more stories of you being young and superiorly stupid."

Knight laughed softly. "I'll keep that in mind."

"Although, now I'm thinking about things, you weren't exactly perfect tonight."

"I'd question whether I'm perfect any night, but continue."

"The zinfandel?"

"Ah."

"I mean, thank fuck. But also, bit of a dick move to swap the gifts without telling me."

Knight shifted, knee bumping Lake's leg. "You're right. I should never have gone over your head like that."

"So why did you?"

"I suppose, I had this *delightful urge* to see relief wash over your face."

Lake grumbled. "What if I hadn't been relieved?"

"I took my chances."

"You must think you know me very well, to take that risk."

"I like to think I know you very well." Knight squeezed their fingers. "But that doesn't excuse not discussing it with you."

Lake hummed, pretending to think about it. "You're forgiven."

"So easily?"

"You being wrong gives me unrivaled pleasure."

Knight snorted, and his laugh rumbled through Lake.

"Besides," Lake hauled in a deep breath and let it out. "What I did was way worse. I shouldn't have gotten involved. Should never have meddled in their love lives. You warned me, and I didn't listen, and I'm so embarrassed."

Heat burned his cheeks.

Knight untangled their fingers, skin sliding off skin, and

Lake immediately missed the warmth. Not that he deserved that comfort right now—

An arm wrapped around him and pressed against the small of his back. Lake instinctively folded against Knight, ducking his head under Knight's chin, arms snuggled up against Knight's silky-haired chest.

Knight rubbed his shoulder blades, down his sensitive flank, over the top of his ass and up again. It felt so good and safe.

Lake blurted against Knight's clavicle, "I convinced Harry they had something. He wasn't sure Philip really liked him, and I told him he totally did. I wanted him to crush on someone that wasn't a direct relative . . . and I'm not even sure I'm right about that, either. I'm the crappiest friend."

A consoling murmur tickled through his hair. Was that the press of lips against his head?

He nudged his leg between Knight's until Knight gave in with a sigh that tickled Lake's scalp and sandwiched his knee.

"I have to tell him tomorrow." Lake never wanted tomorrow to come. "Could we just stay like this forever?"

"Unfortunately not."

Lake started to roll back, but Knight tightened his embrace at his back, around his leg. Lake resettled against him, trying not to make his relief obvious.

"We can, however," Knight said, "enjoy it for a while."

Lake stared at his fingers, playing with the chest hair between Knight's pecs. He had no idea when he'd started doing that. Had Knight noticed?

Should he stop?

He drew spirals over Knight's chest. Lake liked the feeling too much to stop. "I promise, I'll never matchmake again."

Knight hummed non-committedly, like he didn't quite believe it.

"I mean it. Taylor and Amy had to be a fluke. Love and

me? We aren't meant to be. My past relationships have been evidence enough." Lake stifled a frustrated growl against Knight's chest. "What is wrong with me?"

"Nothing is wrong with you."

"But there is, because during this entire conversation wrapped in your arms, at the back of my mind, I've been wondering why I'm not a ten."

Knight chuckled.

"Don't laugh, it's terrible. I thought I didn't care about looks. Apparently, I do."

"You're human."

"If I'm human, what are you? You'd never think something so selfish."

Knight's hand stopped roaming his back. "Shush, you don't know what you're talking about."

"You think selfish things? Like what?"

Knight's lips definitely touched his forehead this time. "Like how glad I am you're having this little meltdown in my arms."

A bit gloating, a little mean-spirited maybe, but completely understandable.

Lake laughed at his own utter stupidity, which quickly morphed into a dismayed groan. "I have to work with Philip, but I don't ever want to see him again. I guess that's part of the lesson. Fuck it'll be awkward. We'll probably pretend like nothing happened, while we're both agonizing over it. Philip feeling rejected, me feeling the full extent of my mistake and being saddened at how shallow he is, and I am. And—"

Lake cut himself off with a curse.

He yanked the blanket, wrapping it like a taco around them.

"And, what?" Knight asked.

"This is my cocoon. I'm not leaving until I emerge a butterfly. Which isn't possible, so I'm gonna stay here the rest of my life, okay?"

"And, what?" Knight insisted, lips twitching into a smile.

"It's not funny."

"I beg to differ."

Lake tweaked Knight's nipple and in one swift move, he was on his back, Knight pressed on top of him—naked toes, meaty thighs, firm chest, semi-hard groin meshing against Lake's.

The glint in Knight's eye stole Lake's breath.

Seeing Knight's lips made his own tingle. The dark, his heightened emotion, and the lure of the forbidden slid tantalizing fingers around them, daring Lake to taste Knight again.

He breathed in sharply and lifted his eyes to Knight's deeply curious ones. "And, what?"

It took effort to look away. Lake sagged into the mattress. Lust was the last thing he should be entertaining.

Regretfully, he pushed at Knight's chest; Knight immediately rolled off him. A sad sound escaped Lake at the loss, and he covered it by clearing his throat. "And I have to tell Harry."

15

Lake stirred, smacking his lips. He'd drooled over his silky pillow.

He shifted an inch and breathed in deeply, nuzzling all that hair.

His eyes pinged open.

Sunlight blinded him and he blinked, adjusting to the brightness. He was wrapped around Knight like an octopus, every limb, toe, elbow, and hair follicle suctioned onto him.

Slowly, he tilted his head up.

Knight had one arm behind his head, the other holding *Moby Dick*. His gaze swept along the lines of the book as if riveted.

He paused, catching Lake's eye. "Good morning."

Bit by bit, Lake unglued himself from Knight. "You're awake and you willingly let me slobber all over your chest?"

"You were sleeping so peacefully, I didn't want to disturb you."

"But you hate it when I suck water straight from the faucet. How can you stand *this*?"

Knight set the book on the bedside table. "*This* cannot be compared."

"I know, it's worse. I should wake up depressed about last night. Not worrying if I've repulsed you."

"Trust me, I feel anything but repulsed."

That sounded decidedly honest and tender. Although, of course Knight meant it sensibly. No one could control themselves while sleeping, and drooling was natural. Nothing to be ashamed of.

"Fine," Lake said. "I won't apologize."

"I wouldn't accept it if you did."

"Ugh, you're too much in the morning."

"Me?" Knight sounded genuinely surprised.

"Yes. You're hyper awake, with no hair out of place, while reading and sanctimoniously telling me it's okay that I dribbled over your nipple."

Knight considered this. "Would it help if I said I ran a hand through my hair?"

"Absolutely not." Lake smirked. "Now I really understand why you're single."

Knight glanced at his wet, matted chest hair. "Back at you."

Lake shoved Knight off the bed, laughter bursting between them.

His surprisingly good mood lasted throughout his morning shower until he bumped into Harry in the kitchen.

Harry, steaming mug in hand, had better color in his cheeks this morning. "How was the party?"

Discomfort wormed in Lake's gut. He barely felt the bite of cool tile on his soles as he padded toward the coffee machine. How did he begin to disappoint Harry? "Um . . . it was . . ."

How could he look at that cute face, clearly hopeful that Lake would share something about Philip missing him, and tell him the truth? "It was fun."

How did Lake live with himself?

"Are you spending another day in bed?" Lake asked.

"I'm feeling better, but . . ." Harry flushed. "Martin's coming by and making me soup. Wants to watch a movie."

Lake eyed Harry's flush, understanding the temptation behind it. Remembering Knight pressed against him, those brown eyes seductive in the dark. "Too much stimulus"—Lake snapped from his deviant thought—"might make your cold come back."

"I'll take it easy. It's been awkward with him since I said I didn't want to return, so this feels like a white flag. Us, just moving on."

Lake nodded. He would *not* interfere. Look where that had gotten him.

Knight swept into the room, dressed in cargo shorts and an old, threadbare shirt. "Ready?"

Not really. He hadn't even started coffee.

But what else were coffee shops for but to avoid telling your friend you fucked up their love life. "Yep, let's go."

They arrived at Tranquil Café before the Sunday rush. Rain droplets slithered down their faces. Knight lifted his shirt, dabbing himself dry, and Lake snorted. A weird nervous response to how sharply his body reacted.

Knight dropped his shirt and eyed him, and Lake beelined toward a free table. Coffee consumed at record speed, he fidgeted with his phone. Knight kept looking at him, like he wanted to say something.

Did he want to know why he'd hurried them out of the house? "I chickened out, okay?"

Knight lifted a brow.

"Telling Harry. Isn't that what you're wondering?"

Knight frowned into his cup. "Not even close." He looked up. "You will have to tell him though. Better from you than from Philip."

Lake cringed, and grabbed his phone.

Knight nabbed it from him, chuckling. "Not via text."

"He's going to hate me."

"Harry is one of the kindest guys I've met. I find that hard to believe."

Lake's phone buzzed. *West* flashed on the screen.

Lake greedily grabbed his phone back, earning a startled look from Knight. "It's about Taylor's party this Sunday."

"What remarkable enthusiasm. How can I get that too?"

Grinning at Knight, he tapped out a reply. "Be funny, gay and single."

"I'm all those things."

"I'm enthused."

An hour later, they arrived at Lake's cottage stocked with supplies and tools. Four hours after that, stomach twisting, Lake left Knight DIYing to get to the food bank on time. To his utter relief, Philip had swapped his shift, so Lake only had his own memories to haunt him through the day.

Exhausted, Lake picked up a mortar-dusted Knight and drove home, the fun prospect of talking to Harry occupying his mind.

"I won't hold back this time. Won't procrastinate. I'll confess that I screwed up. That I misread Philip."

Knight hummed, and Lake shot him a look.

"What does that mean?"

"This is a sixty zone. You're going thirty."

Lake's stomach jumped with nerves with every ounce of pressure he applied to the gas. "Okay, okay, okay. The faster we're home, the faster I'm done."

"That's the right attitude."

"This is the worst day of my life."

"You'll feel lighter once Harry knows."

Lighter? Hmpf. "I'll feel like throwing myself under a train."

"Are you just being dramatic, or dramatic *and* referencing Tolstoy?"

"You did see the bookmark in *Moby Dick* this morning, right? That should tell you everything."

"Interesting choice of bookmark. Large and shaped remarkably like a tabloid magazine."

Lake grinned. "Blame Cameron. He made me buy it. I have to get my Ask Adam fix before they quit the column."

"Riveting reading," Knight said drily.

"Don't dis it until you try it."

"All right then, I will."

"Really?"

"Sure."

"You'll get addicted, I promise."

Knight pointed out the windshield. "Taking the bridge will get us home faster."

Lake reluctantly changed lanes. "I hate you."

A delighted laugh. "Would it be easier if you had something to look forward to after?"

"I don't know," Lake grumbled.

"What if we went to dinner? Something special."

"Something special might need to include high-quality napkins for sobbing into."

"If they don't, I'll let you use my shirt."

"The one you're wearing?"

"No restaurant would let me in like this. I'll shower and change while you break the news to Harry."

Lake glanced down at his jeans and T-shirt. "Will I be okay like this?"

"You could wear a sack and still get service."

That tugged a grin out of Lake. "You know what?"

"What?"

"You're right. Looking forward to dinner will make this easier."

His confession to Harry swamped him with burning hot shame, and the dejection that crested Harry's face . . . Lake would never forgive himself.

They were in Harry's room, sitting against a wall of pillows. The window was cracked open, but it didn't disguise the lingering scent of aftershave that didn't belong to Harry.

Other evidence of Martin's visit peppered the room. A half-empty soup bowl on the bedside table, a stack of books on the desk, and a vibrant bouquet on the window seat.

"Philip didn't like me at all?"

"I'm so sorry," Lake said, unsure if he should pat Harry on the back. Lake had loved that intimacy from Knight, but with Harry it didn't feel comfortable. Their friendship wasn't at that level.

He patted a soft *there-there* on his shoulder, arm well extended. "This is all my fault."

Harry shook his head. "It's not. It's fine. I'm used to it. Philip was out of my league anyway." Harry's smile wobbled.

Lake wanted him to yell and curse him for meddling in the first place. "You're so much better."

"You're too nice, Lake." Harry sighed. "This day has all-around sucked. Martin was robotically good to me. He came and heated the soup, but he never looked in my eyes. He seemed sad, even as he was tenderly taking care of me. He refused to watch the movie from my bed, pulled up a chair instead."

"Maybe it was more comfortable that way?" Lake tried, cringing.

"He's upset that I pushed him away, and I feel . . . ugh. And now this Philip thing . . ." Harry lifted his chin. "Is there ice cream in the freezer?"

"We're out of ice cream but, I mean, um, how do you feel about going out for dinner? Someplace special?"

"Wow, Knight. When you said special, you really meant it."

The view overlooked an archway of fairy-lit cherry-trees, and chandeliers hung gloriously over the three sets of knives and forks either side of his starter platter.

Good thing Lake had insisted on changing into a button-up after eyeballing the nicely dressed Knight emerging from his room.

Even Harry had changed—albeit into his strawberry-print shirt.

"They have some of the best food in the city," Knight murmured. "I only scored a table because I know the owner. I've invested heavily in the restaurant."

Lake sat next to Knight, opposite Harry. Scoping the room, Harry leaned in. "This place is full of couples. We're the only threesome in here."

Knight stared at his beautifully designed beef carpaccio sprigged with parsley that Lake had been eying. "Yes, well. I'm all kinds of entertained by you joining us."

Lake squeezed Knight's knee under the table, eliciting a surprise thigh flex. Knight was so kind to Harry. Always boosted his morale. And when Lake had quietly worried Harry couldn't afford this place, Knight had said he'd always intended to cover dinner.

Knight meant well. But the worried way Harry glanced around . . . were there too many reminders of not having a relationship?

"Is being here making you sad?" Lake asked. "The napkins are high thread-count linen if you need to cry, and if you run out, Knight's shirt looks very crisp."

Harry shook his head, giggling. "I'm fine. Just touched that you'd take me out to make me feel better."

Lake hoped it worked, but he'd find other ways over the next week to keep Harry's mind off Philip.

"This fish and lemon sculpture thing looks . . . delicate," Lake said, prodding the base of his appetizer.

Knight scooped a delicious looking morsel of beef onto his fork, and Lake followed its path towards Knight's mouth. The fork stopped moving.

"Would you like to try, Lake?"

Lake leaned close and parted his lips. Knight didn't hesitate, and the cool slide of the fork on his bottom lip quickly gave way to an explosion of flavor on his tongue. The beef melted in his mouth, and he moaned like he'd never get enough.

Knight's eyes followed every shift of his mouth, and then shot away. "So. Harry. Tell me, who are your biggest influencers?"

Knight engaged Harry in conversation, and Lake might have felt left out if Knight hadn't made up for it by quietly swapping their plates.

For their main meal, Lake promised himself not to eye Knight's (always) superior choice, and mostly managed.

Nevertheless, Knight left him a forkful of sage risotto and tender beef, and Lake could've cried at how amazing it tasted. When dessert came, any restraint on Lake's part was lost, and he whimpered at the beautiful sight of Knight's crème brûlée, berries, and roasted peach ice cream.

Knight laughed under his breath, and directed the waiter to set his dessert at Lake's place, taking Lake's caramel panna cotta instead.

Food eased Harry's disappointment, but it didn't erase it completely. When they returned home Harry made hurried excuses to turn in, and Lake wallowed in the bitterness of his meddling mistake while Knight made chamomile tea and disappeared to bed.

What else could Lake do? Thankfully Philip wasn't part of

Harry's usual circles. At least they wouldn't see each other again. Lake wouldn't be inviting him to Taylor's return party.

Maybe helping organize for Taylor's return would occupy Harry's mind? Or giving him another monologue to practice?

Lake readied himself for bed, brushed his teeth, and knocked on Knight's door. Knight called him in.

Knight's bedroom was bigger than his and continued the farmhouse theme. The walls were dark grey with a white ceiling and window trim and beautiful exposed wooden beams that matched his dresser, the large trunk at the end of the bed, and the two perfectly symmetrical bedside tables.

The bed itself was large with a padded headboard, and set on a soft, medallion-print rug.

Knight was sitting on the side closest to the windows, pillows bunched behind his back. His night lamp stretched light warmly over his naked torso, tanned arms and gently quizzical face.

Knight lay his Kindle on his lap and locked his hands behind his head. Dark tufts of armpit hair and the flex of his pecs stole Lake's attention as he slunk toward the bed.

"Can I help you with something?" Knight asked.

"I don't know." Lake hesitated, then pulled back the blankets and slid into the cool, taut sheets. "I want someone to talk to."

The bed felt divine. He sidled closer to Knight and leaned against the same hill of pillows.

Knight lowered his voice. "Talk about what?"

"Nothing."

"Fascinating conversation."

"Shhh, you're ruining it." Lake let out a tired yawn.

Blankets shifted, replaced by a waft of cool air as Knight swung out of the bed.

"Where are you going?"

Knight padded to the bathroom and returned thirty seconds later with Lake's copy of *Moby Dick*.

Lake groaned. "I can't."

More air swished around him and blankets resettled over his lap. Knight's arm bumped his as he studiously pulled out Lake's tabloid bookmark.

He stopped at the Ask Adam section.

Lake read quietly at Knight's shoulder.

My brother's best friend walked in on me jerking off in the shower, and now that's all I can think about when I touch myself.

My secret crush wants to room with me over the summer. I'm worried about his Jock-ass breaking my antique vases. Worried about his Jock-dick breaking me.

He abducted me one snowy night, let me go the next day, three years later, my blind date is him. I want to run hard and fast. But something is telling me to see him again.

My best friend and his girlfriend invited me into their bed. He only had eyes for me. Now things are awkward. I don't want to lose my friend, want things to go back the way they were. But I've never felt so connected.

"Well," Knight said, carefully folding the tabloid and setting it aside. "I feel reassured."

"Reassured?" Were they reading the same thing?

"Clearly I'm not the only one capable of getting myself into implausible situations."

"What implausible situation—ohh, you mean with out-of-bounds Paul. Maybe you should write your own letter." Lake narrowed his eyes on Knight opening *Moby Dick*. "You're going to make me read it, aren't you? Gonna spout something like fair's fair."

Knight side-eyed him. "Fair *is* fair."

He read aloud.

An hour later, Lake didn't want him to stop.

Knight set it aside with a haughty smile. "See, not so bad."

Lake huffed. "You could read the dictionary and I would like it."

"We can start on that next."

Lake rolled onto his side. He grabbed a pillow that thwarted his view of Knight's face and tossed the offending object to the floor. "I'm truly done. Telling Harry, that amazing food, not to mention the exertion of laying all that kitchen tile. Quite the workout."

"For your eyes," Knight mused.

Heat trickled into Lake's cheeks. "You caught me peeking, huh?"

"Staring seems a more accurate description."

"It's your fault."

"Is it?"

"Seeing you naked and feeling the constant ghost of your let-me-prove-a-point kiss on my lips opened Pandora's box."

Knight tucked a finger under Lake's chin and urged Lake to look at him. "I didn't want to bring you trouble."

"Well now I have the urge to look for more of it."

"With me?"

Lake shut his eyes. "Oh my God, it's so wrong and Taylor will freak. But I cannot stop imagining kissing you. I don't even know why, because you frustrate me. On a daily basis. And I know you're in love with Paul, and that anything with my best friend's dad is wrong, but I'm thinking about it. Hell, I've been more than thinking about it."

His eyes shot open. "Oh God, toss me out of your bed right now."

He started to push himself out, but Knight firmly palmed his waist, splayed fingers warm against him. "Stay right where you are."

"It's stupid lust. I promise to control myself."

"Are you sure it's only lust?"

Lake froze, frightened at any other possibility, and violently shook his head. Knight didn't need this nonsense from him, no matter how stoically he was taking it. "You're more than Taylor's dad to me, you're my friend, and I don't want stupid physical urges to change that. Can we please pretend this conversation never happened?"

"No."

"No? Why not? You can't exactly be enjoying it."

"Not all parts of it." Knight let out a deep breath. He looked crushingly sad and frustrated, but a wealth of patience quickly cloaked that. "I don't think you know what you want."

"In general? Or in regards to my love life?"

"Sometimes, I want to dive into your head and help you figure everything out, but you need to make your own discoveries."

"I trust you. Whatever your insights are, they're probably right. You may as well tell me."

"I can't and won't force them."

"Fine, and I apologize for any future ogling. I'll try to stop."

Knight pressed a light, tingling kiss at the corner of Lake's lips. "Ogle away, Emerett. I'm extremely flattered."

He turned off his lamp, sinking the room into darkness.

"Knightly?"

"Yes?"

"Thank you for today."

"You're welcome."

"Willing to make time for others. That's one of those seventeen—nope, that's one of your *countless* virtues."

Knight's pinkie slid against his. "Any time, Lake."

"Your bed is so comfortable." How did he ask if he could stay? "Like, super comfy."

"Sleep here. I took it for granted you would."

"You did?"

"Shhh. Good night."

Lake smiled. "Good night."

Lake: West won't make it to the barbecue Sunday.

Taylor: He said he wouldn't miss it.

Lake: Sorry.

Taylor: Oh. Well. . . . Gotta catch a taxi, almost home. See you tm.

Lake dipped a spoon into the chicken-and-cashew curry simmering on the stove and hummed in appreciation as he tasted the spicy flavors. "This is the kind of food that makes me feel better after a shitty week of boring work. Today was hell. I'm glad I made it in time."

Knight batted his spoon away from a second dip.

"This is for Taylor and Amy." Lake sneaked around his other side and tried again. "Oy, what are you doing?"

"I swapped the spoon, at least. C'mon."

"If you're hungry, make yourself a piece of bread, like I did."

Lake gazed at the open jar of tarry-looking chocolate spread and half-eaten slice of bread. "This curry is so good, though." Lake jerked a finger toward Taylor's kitchen window. "Hey, they're here."

Knight didn't take the bait.

"You've already eaten half their dinner, I'd prefer if you didn't eat the other half."

"You're embellishing."

"No double-dipping. Why can't you respect my kitchen?"

"Because it's not your kitchen."

"You know what I mean."

"I do respect your kitchen. It's your perfectly delicious cooking that's the real evil here."

"I'll cook for you and Harry at home. Just hold out an hour, and if you've stocked the fridge, water the plants."

Lake more or less did what he was told, and returned to Knight pulling out a fresh loaf of bread from the oven.

Some very nice buns on display. . .

He suppressed electric shivers by absorbing all the Taylor-ness of this house. The last time Lake had been here—watering potted plants not included—he and Taylor had hung out together in silence on the sofa. At some point he'd rolled off and made himself a sandwich, tossing Taylor a mini muffin. Then, when Lake was on the toilet, they'd had a great back and forth on their phones.

Tomorrow, his best friend was back.

This was good.

This was *great.*

Lake swallowed a nervous lump in his throat and wiped his clammy palms over his thighs.

Why did he feel so anxious about seeing Taylor? Was he worried their dynamics had changed now he was married? Or was he afraid his illicit thoughts about Taylor's dad might be obvious, and awkward, and—

That one.

Lake hopped onto the counter next to the stove. "Are you looking forward to Taylor being back?"

One firm hand landed flat against his outer thigh. "You'll burn yourself." Knight nudged him aside. "I've missed my boy."

"Yeah, I mean." Lake nodded profusely. "Me too. Obviously."

Knight looked up sharply, and Lake gulped.

"Really missed him," Lake said, picking up a salt grinder and fiddling with the top knob. "I guess I won't be in your hair as much."

"How do you figure?" Knight's voice quivered, surprised. "Taylor and Amy will want their space, and I can't see you happy being a third wheel at their house. Your cottage is on the market. Unless you've found a better place to stay, I imagine things will—thankfully—stay as they are."

Thankfully? "You don't mind?"

"I more than don't mind, Lake. You make the place feel like home."

"Um, really?" Lake set the salt shaker aside and scrubbed his face. "I mean, I feel like it's home too." His admission poured out, "I'm nervous about Taylor coming back. I love him and everything, but there's something . . . Like, what if he thinks I spend too much time with you? What if he doesn't like it? What if you have to stop hanging out with me?"

Knight settled his palms on Lake's knees and met his eyes. "Let's cross those bridges as we get to them. Taylor is a grown man. He understands that relationships evolve. We'll find our new balance. Pass me the salt?"

Lake passed it to him. "What if the balance makes someone unhappy? Maybe I shouldn't live with you."

Knight ground a mountain of salt into the curry. "Let's not be hasty. Let's focus on seeing Taylor again. His party."

"All right. What are you gonna sing?"

Knight finally put the grinder down. "When have you ever seen me sing?"

"Come on. I dare you. Your voice would be good for a deep 'Love Shack.' I'm thinking of doing the classic, crime-if-it's-not-done, '500 Miles'."

"I'll never get sick of it. Even if I've heard you sing it 10,000 times."

"It makes me think of you, you know."

Knight stopped stirring. "Really?"

"You walk everywhere, all the time. Hell, you made us walk here. You'd be the kind of guy who really would walk five-hundred miles—and five-hundred more—for, you know, Taylor. Or Paul. Or, you know. Me."

Knight resumed stirring. "You know I'd walk five-hundred miles for you?"

"I hope you would? I would too. You know, for Taylor. Or you."

"I'm looking forward to hearing this song more than I thought."

Lake laughed. "You have to sing too. It'd crack me up, but also it'd make Taylor feel better. I think he's disappointed that West won't show."

"West won't show?"

"He said something came up. It's a pity. I was looking forward to meeting him."

Knight hit the wooden spoon a few tight times against the side of the pot, freeing it of curry. "You were?"

"He seems interesting. I'm curious if he's just as interesting in person. But I guess not this time."

Knight spoke coolly, "This is just like him."

Lake stared questioningly at Knight's apparent annoyance.

Knight's face pinched. "He did this a lot at high school."

Lake agreed West not coming sucked, but—through texts from West himself and Taylor—he'd learned a lot about West over the last week, and he had the itching desire to play devil's advocate. To argue with Knight. "His parents sound homopho-bic. Maybe they had something to do with him not coming?"

"I accepted that he didn't come because of me when he was at school, but he's a grown man now."

"Wow, what's he done to make you so prickly?"

Knight cleared his throat. "He's always making promises and then cancelling last minute. It always made Taylor feel crappy."

"Taylor's also a grown man now, remember? He doesn't need you to hate West for him."

"I don't hate West. I just haven't seen any proof of him caring about my son."

"Easily said. But you should know how hard it is for some guys to juggle the love they have for their parents and the love they have for men."

"I walked out on my parents when they demanded I give Taylor up for adoption. Sometimes you have to make hard choices."

"Not everyone works like you do. You taking Taylor was brave and admirable, but whatever West is enduring is not the same situation. You can't know how much this might tear him up. How much he's holding back being himself because he loves his mum and dad. Or needs them. Or both."

"If he cared enough about Taylor, he'd have found a way to sneak around."

"You're determined to dislike him."

Knight turned his back to Lake, washing dishes in the sink. "He isn't considerate or respectful."

Lake hummed thoughtfully. He wasn't sure if Knight was pissed at West, or at the situation. Maybe Knight had had a shitty work week too?

"If you were West, I'm sure you'd have handled it better. You'd have snuck around to Taylor's party as promised. But maybe West informing me that he couldn't make it was the most respect he could manage."

"He left *you* to break it to Taylor instead of explaining to Taylor himself."

Lake laughed robustly and jumped off the counter. The impact of the tile on his heels vibrated to his brain.

"You really don't like him." He grabbed a dish towel and started drying the spoons he'd used. "He seemed nice in his texts."

Knight harrumphed.

"You haven't seen him in years. He'd have changed since high school."

"Possibly."

"He seems like a smart, driven guy with a lot of personality. His texts read like he could charm the pants off anyone."

Knight's jaw twitched, and the drain gurgled.

No point arguing. Knight clearly wouldn't change his mind about the poor guy. But this stubbornness and dislike didn't feel like the Knight that Lake knew. The Knight he knew understood other perspectives. Empathized.

His friend was imperfect after all.

He slung the dish towel over his shoulder and grabbed his trusty spoon. "Not for the curry," Lake promised. "For the chocolate spread."

He beelined for the open jar.

Knight frowned. "That's not . . . try it first. On some bread."

Lake snorted and dipped his spoon in, really dunking it, scooping heaps of thick, dark chocolate. He wouldn't lose his appetite for dinner.

Knight gave in and leaned against the sink, shaking his head.

Lake made a show of lifting the spoon to his mouth and opened wide—

A nasty explosion of taste hit his tongue.

He bolted to the sink, shoving Knight's grinning ass aside, and spat it out. "Oh my God what kind of chocolate is that?"

"Carob. Amy's caffeine intolerant."

"That poor, poor woman." He spat again. "Jesus. Where were your hand slaps when I needed them?"

A gentle smack hit his ass. Lake knew he'd feel its warmth the rest of the evening. "Come on," Knight said. "We'll get some dinner into you."

17

"That last flight was the worst I've had in my life," Taylor said. Lake, Taylor, Harry, and Cameron were lounging around Cameron's backyard pool under large umbrellas. "Turbulence the whole way."

"Hey, no complaining." Lake flicked water at Taylor, who laughed and flicked some back, spraying Lake's neck and cheek. Pleasantly cool in this heat. "You traveled Europe while the rest of us dragged ourselves to work."

"No dragging on my side," Cameron said, sipping iced tea. He sat on the edge of the pool in a baggy T-shirt, legs dipping. "I love Mondays."

Taylor leaned his head against the side of the pool while the rest of him floated. "I'm looking forward to working again too."

"Did you find it hard not working for so long?"

Taylor and Cameron chatted about their jobs while Lake wished his lemonade had something stronger in it. Enough of people loving their work.

Harry's pinched face suggested he wasn't keen on the conversation either. Understandably, on the heels of another failed audition. God, even in the shade it looked like he was burning.

He grabbed Harry by the arm and pulled him deeper into the shade.

Taylor watched, his brow flickering. He'd want to know why his cousin-in-law was staying at his dad's; Lake hoped he could give him a rundown without bringing up the Philip palaver. "Is Amy coming for a dip?"

"Nope," Taylor said. "She got even less sleep on the plane than I did. She's napping."

"We'll catch up later then. At your place. While you're giving me the gifts that you poured your heart into finding for me."

Taylor fanned a leg over the surface and kicked Lake gently in the stomach. "It's good to see you're still the same."

"You weren't gone *that* long. Nothing's changed at all."

"Ohh," Harry chirped, pointing towards Cameron's side gate. "Knightly's joining us."

A tan towel was draped over his shoulder, exposing that glorious torso.

Lake heaved himself out of the pool, spraying water all over the burning concrete path as he darted toward the gate. Their gazes caught and Knight stopped moving. Lake shoved through the gate, flattened his damp palms over that firm, silky chest, and pushed Knight deeper down the shady side of the house.

The soles of his feet found relief on cool brick, but that was the only relief he felt.

Knight's eyebrows lifted, waiting.

"You can't."

"Why not? Taylor asked me to come, and I doubt Cameron has any objections."

"I have objections."

"To spending an afternoon with my son?"

"No. Yes. I mean . . ." Lake growled in frustration. "It's asking for a lot of . . . control."

Brown eyes darkened. Was that . . . understanding?

"Control," Knight murmured.

Lake's fingers were still pressed against Knight, threading through his chest hair. He dropped his hands and glanced away. "You're practically naked, and I can't quite help. . ." That intense zipping attraction was already walking over him, leaving goose bumps behind.

He shoved a nervous hand through his hair. "Taylor will notice."

"Ah."

"Maybe I should leave." Lake started to march past, and Knight braced a cool, firm hand around his shoulder.

"Your sudden disappearance will also raise questions. I'll go."

"Really?"

Knight's soft gaze sparkled in Lake's chest, and—problematically—lower. Knight whipped his towel from his shoulder and wrapped it around his waist.

From over the fence, Cameron cried out, "Are you guys coming in?"

Still bracing Lake's shoulder, Knight raised his voice, drenched in urgency. "Goddammit. Something stung me."

Air fizzled out of Lake. "Shit. Are you okay? Should I call an ambulance? Prepare your death bed?"

That earned him a glare and a pinched shoulder-squeeze before Knight released him. "I'll be fine. Probably should put something on it."

Lake retreated, blowing him a kiss. "Call if you need anything."

He dropped back into the cool pool next to Harry, who was fanning himself. Taylor looked at him, yawning. "Dad okay?"

"Just a little sting. All good."

"What were you chatting about before the bee?" Cameron asked, because he was Cameron. "Seemed pretty hush-hush."

Lake floundered, spewing the first thought that popped into his head. "I can't tell you, it's a surprise."

Cameron looked startled, albeit thrilled. When he left to

refill his iced tea, Taylor swam across to Lake. God, now he and Knight had to concoct a surprise.

"You and dad are surprising Cameron?"

Let's go with that. "Uh huh."

"What are you teaming up to surprise him about?"

"On, um . . . for getting the rights to make the Ask Austen program for his channel. He didn't tell you? Ask him, I'm sure he'll keep you entertained all afternoon. But yeah, we're throwing him and his whole . . . team a party. Ask-Austen themed. Next weekend. Still working out the invitations, though."

"Ask-Austen themed?"

Lake nodded with a stiff smile. "Everyone will be sent a contemporary dilemma and at the party, we have to match everyone's dilemma to a piece of Austen advice."

"Amy will love it."

"Um, yeah. I mean, it'll be fun. But let's keep it on the down low. First I want to enjoy your barbecue tomorrow. There'll be karaoke."

Taylor hissed. "Thank you for the heads up. I'll bring ear plugs."

Despite Lake's worries, having Taylor back was easy. They found their groove and the afternoon raced by, followed by the evening.

Lake tried not to look in Knight's direction when he arrived with takeout. And, even though he'd done it a thousand times in front of Taylor, he didn't swap his Malai Kofta for Knight's Tandoori Chicken.

They spent the hour after dinner in Taylor and Amy's darkened living room, looking at pictures projected onto the wall and hearing amazing stories of misadventure.

All too soon, the lights came on again. Lake felt Knight's eyes on him.

Did Lake have to undrape himself from the couch and

leave the happy couple to themselves? Was that really necessary?

On the smaller sofa, arm curled around Amy, Taylor laughed. "I know that look, Dad." He glanced at Lake. "It's time to leave."

Knight said, "It is getting late, and you both . . . well."

Was Knight blushing faintly at the thought of his son being intimate?

Lake smirked. "Probably a good idea to leave the love birds."

Knight threw him a cautionary look.

It probably didn't say much about the graciousness of his character that Lake was laughing inside. Laughing, and itching to make Knight squirm. "Staying longer would be encroaching—"

Knight strode over and pulled Lake to his feet with startling ease. Lake laughed. "Hey."

"We'll see you at the barbecue tomorrow," Knight said pleasantly to Taylor and Amy.

"Sure thing, Dad."

Knight ushered Lake out of the house, and Lake tossed a goodbye over his shoulder.

Outside, in the fresh early-summer breeze, Knight softly clapped the back of Lake's head. "Really, Lake?"

"Hey, I didn't do anything."

Another chastising look. "That's my son."

"And adult, married sons don't get intimate?"

"No—Yes. I'd just prefer not to make a thing of it. Bedroom affairs are private."

"Bedroom affairs. I'm still shocked you didn't call it your manhood or member. And, holy shit, now I'm wondering if you're prudish in bed. If you've ever had one night stands, or if you only have sex after forging a deeper connection—and I'm gonna run home now."

Lake started to hoof it and Knight snagged his shirt, holding him back. "Are you asking if I have sex just for the sake of it?" Lake looked at him, which took a little more courage than normal. "I prefer to know—and actually like—a guy, but occasionally release is the ultimate goal."

The walk back was quiet, but Lake couldn't shake the restlessness that itched under his skin. Instead of heading to bed, Knight stole into the backyard to water the garden.

Lake resisted the urge to follow and found Harry in the living room, kneeling on the hearth, ripping paper out of a diary and throwing it into the fireplace.

"What are you doing?" Lake perched on the arm of the upholstered chair beside him.

"Purging myself of old, unrequited feelings."

Lake sighed guiltily. This thing with Philip had affected Harry more than he thought. "I'm not sure the fireplace actually works."

Harry slumped onto his heels. "Right."

"Do you want to, er, chat about it?"

Harry shook his head, miserable. "I'll just binge-watch Netflix."

Lake had no interest in Harry's selection. Though he did stay, for half an hour. When another wildlife documentary started, Lake exaggerated a yawn and wished him good night.

Upstairs, he grabbed his laptop and slung himself onto Knight's bed.

It really was more comfortable.

Steps padded in the hall.

"Lake?" Knight called out.

"In here."

Knight entered his room. "What are you doing?"

Lake gestured toward his open laptop. "Curating a list of films for us to watch. *Much Ado About Nothing*, *Pride and Prejudice*, *To Kill A Mockingbird*, and a dozen others."

"You're doing what?"

"Curating. Come check it out yourself, you poor confused man."

Knight sat on the bed. "This is a list of the books you said you'd read."

"Yeah. I know."

"Why would you watch them?"

"Because they exist as a film?"

"Yes, but watching defeats the purpose."

"Oh, sorry. I didn't realize the purpose was to spend weeks boring myself."

Knight ducked out of the room and returned drumming his fingers over *Moby Dick*. "Bunch over, I'll read to you."

Lake clapped his laptop shut. "I was wondering what it would take to make you offer."

Knight cast him an ill-amused look. "Had you considered asking?"

"Too pathetic. This way, I simultaneously set up a plan B."

"That is strangely crafty of you."

"Yes, and that curated list is there whenever you've had enough."

"The pressure is on."

Lake closed his eyes, absorbing Knight's calming voice. When he turned the page to start a second chapter, Lake rolled onto his side, stopping him. Knight's forearm flexed under his palm, and brown eyes turned to him, heavy with the late hour.

Lake's mouth dried. "Thank you for faking the bee sting earlier."

"I understood."

"I was more in control at Taylor and Amy's."

"You barely looked at me."

"Which was why I was more in control." Lake rolled onto his back, grimacing at the ceiling. "This is terrifying." He swallowed. "Thank you for . . . you know, being cool about it."

ANYTA SUNDAY

Knight rolled to face him, and the closeness thrummed through Lake. Knight drew in a breath to respond—

"By the way, we have to host an Ask Austen party for Cameron."

Knight scrubbed his jaw, all gorgeous lines and intense presence. "A party for Cameron?"

Lake explained his earlier conundrum. ". . . So we have to invite everyone Cameron works with for an evening acting out forbidden and questionable scenarios."

A warm, tutting laugh. "You have a troubling knack for forging ahead without checking yourself."

"What else was I supposed to say?"

"I don't know, tell him we were discussing when we'd do the weekly shopping, or who left the wet towel on the bathroom floor."

Lake scowled. "Do you ever let anything go? I did that *one* time."

Knight grew louder with disbelief. "I pick up your towel every other day."

"Well that must be annoying," Lake said, voice still haughtily raised. "I will do better."

"Thank you!"

"You're welcome!"

Knight bubbled into a laugh, and Lake joined him before reluctantly dragging himself to his own bed. "Maybe this is why we're both single."

Knight's laughter simmered to a smile. "It's certainly why I am."

130

18

L ake found himself manning the grill. Not so much because he wanted to be helpful, but because it had a great vantage point over the garden and everyone in it. The sun settled low on the horizon, and the thirty-odd guests mingled in the golden light. In the gazebo, Harry sang on the Karaoke machine with a rapt Martin as his audience; Cameron was at the drinks station pouring them both a beer; Taylor and Amy had disappeared inside the house, and Knight . . .

Lake scoured the garden for him. In the shadows of the apple tree, wearing that burnt-fall red T-shirt and shorts, looking sinfully sexy as he talked with Josh, whose blue hair glowed in a beam of sunshine that filtered through the branches. The conversation held Knight's attention.

Lake's gaze narrowed on the suggestive way Josh lounged against the trunk, the way Knight threw his chin up and laughed. The way he leaned.

"Those sausages are a little burned," Cameron said, holding out a beer.

Lake turned the meat, grabbed his beer, and thrust the tongs into Cameron's hand. "Be an angel and man this for a sec?"

"Sure."

Lake was halfway across the yard, gripping the beer can, liquid splashing over his hand. He paused to take a few gulps.

"There you are." Taylor tackled Lake into a hug from the side.

Lake caught his balance. "I thought you and Amy were . . ."

"A bunch of her girlfriends showed up, so . . ." He laughed. "You have to entertain me."

"You know how much I love being second choice."

Taylor steered them away from Knight and ridiculously smart, gorgeous Josh, and cornered him into the gazebo where Harry was serenading Martin. The sight elicited conflicting emotions in Lake's chest. Concern. Understanding. Guilt.

Maybe he really did love Martin—wait, was that a goodbye song?

"Thanks for this," Taylor said, plunking onto the bench. "Nice seeing everyone again."

"Yeah, cool." No more focusing on Harry. *Not your business!* "Sorry West couldn't make it."

"Maybe next time." Taylor kicked his legs out and crossed his ankles. "You know, I had the strangest dream last night. I walked in on you and my dad in bed. Together."

The can crumpled under Lake's grip and beer spilled out the top. Lake tossed it into the recycling bin. "Really? Weird."

"You were hurrying to get dressed, trying to tell me it wasn't what it looked like."

"I had a dream last night too. You weren't in it. Neither was your dad. It was boring. A reminder how vanilla my life is. How much I play by the rules." All said while Lake was replaying that sneaky forbidden kiss he and Knight had shared a few weeks ago.

Wow, he was a sucky friend.

"You? Vanilla?" Taylor snickered. "Certainly not in my dream. I tell ya, it was enough to scar me for life. Why aren't you laughing?"

"Oh, hahahaha. I totally am. It's . . . hilarious."

Frowning, Taylor looked behind him and back at Lake.

"Okay, now I get it." He shook his head. "I'll never understand that weird one-sided animosity thing you have toward Josh."

"No idea what you're talking about."

"C'mon, anyone can see it. Dad sees it, too."

Lake snapped his attention to Taylor.

Taylor grinned. "He said it's because Josh is gifted the way you'd like to be gifted."

That hit Lake with an ache. "I do not wish I were gifted like him."

Except, the words came out like his conscience had stamped them with "lie."

Sure, Josh was smart and universally liked, but that didn't mean Lake wished he were the one entertaining Knight under the apple tree right now . . .

"Hey, I need another beer, can I get you one?"

Taylor started to stand, and Lake stopped him, tossing him the master Karaoke song list.

"Choose one."

Lake grabbed two chilled beers and meandered toward the gazebo by way of the apple tree. "Oh, there you guys are."

Knight and Josh looked up at Lake as he ducked around a low branch. "How are you doing?"

Josh's smile was bright, with a sincerity that made Lake feel bad about his own fake one. Lake shifted from foot to foot, restless under Knight's shrewd appraisal.

"We were talking about how many New Zealanders are living abroad," Josh said.

Lake had zero to contribute. Oh, wait—"Taylor's old friend West lived in London? Did you ever meet him?"

Josh stuttered briefly, "I-I might have. West . . . now I remember, yes."

What was Knight deducing? Did his attention have to be so narrowed on Lake?

Lake hoped he wouldn't crack the beer cans. "So you can confirm? West's real?"

"He's very real."

"Good, I was starting to think everyone was making him up and I was texting Taylor the whole time as some kind of grand joke."

"Probably not."

"So, tell me. What's he like in person? Charming? Hot?"

Knight made a deep, throaty sound. He shoved off the tree trunk and excused himself to get drinks.

Air stirred around Lake, scented with Knight, and it took great effort not to watch him go.

Josh folded his arms and shrugged. "West is, um, fine."

"Just fine?"

"Yep."

Josh might have a fancy degree, but he was stingy with details. Knight returned two excruciating minutes later, passing Josh a drink. Josh thanked him, and Knight smiled.

Harry's singing stopped. "I think it's time"—he snagged Knight's gaze—"for my traditional song."

Chin up, he headed back to Taylor, passed him both their beers, and took over the Karaoke machine. He tried to lose himself in the rhythm of the song, tried to work his voice as best he could. Josh might be gifted and smart and read lots of books, but Lake knew how to belt out a tune.

Knight rested against the tree, watching him with his usual patient fondness. Lake liked it, but it wasn't enough.

He wanted Knight to . . . to take back what he'd said. About Lake not being as gifted.

He finished singing with a bow, and Taylor and Knight clapped the loudest. That was something, at least.

Feeling marginally better, he set the microphone down and scooped up the beer Taylor held out for him. "Thanks."

"Couldn't stop staring at Josh, could you? If I didn't know better, I'd say you were into him."

Lake laughed—hopefully not too shrilly—and really went to work on his beer. He pulled the can free with a slurp and pointed to Taylor. "Your turn."

Taylor gave an apologetic grin. "Amy snuck away from her girlfriends. She's waiting upstairs . . ."

Lake waved him away. "Go be a husband then."

He finished his beer, helping Harry pick out songs for later. "You're an amazing singer," Harry said, cheeks bunched in a glittery smile. "I loved your voice, your enthusiasm. You stole Knight's attention too."

"You think?"

"Uh huh."

Lake excused himself from Harry and fought the nervous rolling in his belly as he headed back to the apple tree.

Josh was gesturing around the garden, but Knight watched him approach.

Each step riddled him with electricity. God, if it felt like this, he wasn't sure he could do five-hundred miles. He'd combust before that. Hell, a dozen steps, and his palms were sweating.

Knight sipped his soda, still not looking away. The intensity pulled at Lake, raw and arousing, and he was there already.

He stopped abruptly.

Josh seemed surprised at his return too and lost his train of thought. " . . . singing. I might try a song or two myself."

He marched between them and jogged into the gazebo.

"Are you having a good time?" Lake asked.

"Far more than I thought."

"So . . ."

Knight raised a brow. "Yes?"

"We've not really talked all day." Not alone, at least.

Did Knight's focus just drop to Lake's lips?

Lake's heart pounded.

Faintly, he was aware of Taylor in his bedroom, and of his view into the yard, and he shoved his hands into his back pockets and rocked on his heels.

The most beautifully pitched voice sailed over the backyard. Lake—and half the guests—spun toward the gazebo, where Josh gripped the microphone, eyes shut, pouring his soul into Brett Eldredge's "The One You Need."

Well.

Holy crap.

He'd forgotten just how amazing Josh could sing.

Lake clapped reluctantly when it was over, while the rest of the party whistled and encored him. Josh feigned modesty, but quite happily dove into another song.

Knight stood beside him, taking in the show. "He's talented."

God, yes. "I mean, they're not exactly hard songs."

A husky laugh. "Admit it. He's exceptional."

Lake's chest heaved with disappointment—hurt? He folded his arms. "He's not the one I care to see singing."

Lake visualized Knight watching *him* on stage with the same reverence. Imagined Knight's praise warming him . . .

This time his lips pulled into a pained smile when he clapped.

The second encore was too much. "How are you the best at everything?" He sighed.

He wasn't sure, but he thought he heard Knight chuckle.

Josh chose a classic from *Grease*. As soon as the familiar melody started, Josh swung a finger over the gathering party. "Who's gonna come up here and help me sing?"

"You're the one that I want." Knight pressed his soda against Lake, catching his eye. "I feel this one." A secret smile played at his lips as he whisked toward the gazebo, calling for Josh's attention.

Josh tossed him the second mic and Knight caught it deftly.

Hot, burning frustration fired Lake's veins. Look how he thrust his whole body into the song. How he gave it his everything. He gave the Olivia Newton-John parts such a unique spin with his deep voice, it was making him shiver. Truly a magnificent sight, hips bucking seductively in the role, a damn glint in his eye.

The way he sang—to the crowd, to *Josh* . . .

Lake sipped Knight's soda, scowling. It was the hottest act he'd ever seen, and Josh had been the one to lure Knight on stage.

Yep. Lake was a horrible person. Taylor and Knight were right from the beginning.

Lake didn't like Josh at all.

19

G ood looking.

Knightly called Josh *good looking.*

He'd overheard it hours ago, while Josh had been exhibiting his talents in the gazebo. But Lake couldn't let it go.

The guests had left, Taylor and Amy had returned home, Harry was snoring in bed, and Lake was watering scruffy-looking flowers and aloe vera plants. Moonlight settled blueish over the garden and a fresh breeze slanted the grass and the leaves on the apple tree.

It all smelled so . . . Knightly.

He grumbled and continued watering, mentally listing all of Josh's offences.

He was disgustingly, suspiciously perfect. Single. He had many topics on which to converse with Knight. There was an eighteen-year age gap, but it didn't show, physically or intellectually. And, dammit, even Lake had to admit Josh was a better target for Knight's attentions than married Paul.

"There you are."

Lake startled. Knight stopped at his side, hands deep in his short's pockets, staring at the wet brick.

"Here I am," Lake murmured, shifting the spray a couple of feet in the other direction.

"You disappeared for most of the party."

By design. "I hung out with Taylor inside. It was cold out here earlier."

Knight pinned him with a look.

Damn it for being a tropically warm night.

"Well I enjoyed myself," Knight said. "Karaoke was a fantastic idea. Everyone had a good time performing, and I had an even better time watching."

"Glad you liked it," Lake said, smiling tightly.

Knight's voice dropped to a hush. "What are you doing, Emerett?"

Lake shivered. The way his name threaded through him, leaving goosebumps in its wake. He cleared his throat. "I'm watering the garden."

"You are spending a lot of time hosing the weeds . . . at midnight . . . when you've never watered the plants before."

Lake shrugged. But God, Knight's presence radiated toward him. "You love this garden, and I figure, since I've moved in officially, I should help with the domestic chores."

"Look at me?"

Lake did not. "If these are weeds, I suppose I should stop watering them."

He strode toward the tap, shut it off, and found Knight beside him again. "Ugh. Could you not stand so close?"

Knight stepped back, a slight frown creasing his brow. He nodded. "Of course."

So respectful and unquestioning. Knight didn't understand.

Lake wasn't even sure *he* understood.

It just burned, and burned, and burned.

"I wish you'd had a better time tonight," Knight murmured.

He sounded sincere, but also disappointed, and Lake didn't like that.

He was being shitty. His friend had enjoyed himself, maybe even found someone he could foster a relationship with. Lake wanted both those things for Knight. Sure, he was a dad. But dads were allowed intimacy, and more than that—they were allowed to fall in love again.

Josh, was . . . a decent man.

"He is a good looking, exceptionally talented guy. I'm wrong to get jealous."

Knight looked at him, surprised. Pleased. "I wasn't sure you'd recognize it."

"It's boiling something fierce. I'm sorry for turning away from your duet."

"I'm amazed you did. You were the one who wanted me on stage so desperately."

"There's something about Josh that makes me feel . . . less, and he was practically humping you at one point, and I cracked."

Knight smiled. Rather brightly. Although that might have been the moonlight.

He angled his head toward the bench. "Sit with me for a bit?"

They sat, and Lake gritted his teeth at how carefully Knight made sure to give him space. "Jealousy is not contagious, as far as I'm aware."

Knight followed Lake's pointed gaze to the space between them and shifted toward the middle. Lake met him there until their arms pressed lightly together. The spark between them took some of the edge off his mounting frustration.

"Did you hear about Philip?" Knight asked.

"No."

"Cameron told me he hooked up with Trey after he returned to Josh's party last weekend."

"What?"

Knight raised his brows. "I thought you'd be relieved."

"But so quickly? After that whole show about my lemon?"

"Apparently he took it and made lemonade."

Lake squished his face in distaste. "Never mention lemon again. The word's been soured."

Soft vibrations of laughter shuddered through his arm.

Knight's profile was sharp, determined, and confident, like

the man himself. "Thanks. That gossip slightly distracted me from your dalliance with Josh."

Knight faced him. "What would more thoroughly distract you?" His eyes glittered softly in the milky light. "A discussion of Cameron-related business? Or delving into the curious behavior of Martin and Harry—"

Lake kissed him. A rapid jerk of his head and the crush of his eager lips against Knight's surprised ones. Electricity surged through him at the touch, sluggishly followed by sanity.

He pulled back and swallowed the horrified ball in his throat. "God, I'm sorry. It . . . overcame me."

Astonishment—arousal?—flickered in Knight's eyes. Lake drew in a breath and shakily let it out again.

"Oh, Emerett."

Another second of panic seized Lake. He tried to cobble together an excuse, but Knight ran his tongue over the bottom of his lip, and it fried Lake's senses.

The inches between them disappeared; Knight's hands threaded through Lake's hair, cradling his head as their mouths met. Lake sucked in a breath, surprised, and instinctively wound his arms around Knight's neck.

The firm kiss rolled over his lips from one corner to the other.

Knight tasted of dew. Like he belonged outdoors.

A strong hand braced his waist, steering him onto Knight's lap, and Lake folded against Knight's hard body like it was made for him. He groaned and Knight pressed harder against him, everywhere teasing friction. His shorts tightened painfully; the ache kept compounding.

Lips softened, and then slid away, leaving behind a damp line that tickled in the breeze.

"We should stop. We're not thinking clearly."

He leaned in and whispered against the warm shell of Knight's ear. "I thought you weren't always so level-headed?"

Knight slid his hand into Lake's hair and palmed his head, the heel of his hand cushioning his nape. A sharp, wet nip came to his ear, eliciting a ticklish shiver that pooled in Lake's crotch. "Always baiting me . . ."

Lake was lost to sensation. Delirious on it.

"Always losing my mind." He needed more. "Touch me."

Knight pulled up Lake's T-shirt and tugged it off, throwing it over the arm of the bench. Lake's fingers shook like an addict's, yanking Knight's shirt free. His fingers sank into Knight's chest hair, splayed wide.

Maybe giving in just once, getting it out of his system, would help.

Lake breathed the warm night air deep into his lungs. The garden was quiet save the whisper of grass and shifting leaves. The sky stretched over them, deep navy, a few speckled stars, and the crescent glow of moonlight.

Slender white flowers framed the dark pillars of the gazebo, and the hose snaked over the grass where he'd dropped it. The bench squealed, drawing Lake's attention back to Knight, whose eyes darkened with wonder and desire. A nervous fluttering rose from Lake's gut to his chest.

Shivers exploded over his skin.

Whatever they were on the precipice of, Lake needed to jump.

He leaned in and dropped a soft kiss on Knight's lips. A feathery gasp glided over his chin.

Lake's hands roamed Knight's chest, up to his shoulders and down the strong lines of his arms. His thumbs hooked into the crevice between forearm and bicep and he rubbed the sensitive skin.

Knightly. He was doing this with Knightly. His best friend's dad. His biggest critic.

Madness. This was Lake's body betraying him at every level. This was . . . a one-off thing.

Knight's nose slid against Lake's and their mouths met again, hot breaths pebbling together.

"Your kisses are sweet," Lake murmured. "Curiously addictive. What will the rest of you do to me?"

Knight laughed and his lips were back on Lake, firm and frantic, devastating his senses.

The sweep of tongue had Lake mewling for more of Knight's mouth. God, he couldn't even think. Usually he was so aware when he kissed a guy. Usually, he was self-conscious the first time he had sex.

How easy and natural this was with Knight.

Knight knew Lake's faults already, so he could make the wrong move—multiple wrong moves—and Knight would patiently tell him and teach him to make it better.

He ground against Knight, reveling in the hard outline of Knight's cock and the tightening pressure at his hips.

Their bare chests bumped. His left nipple grazed Knight's and their kiss morphed. Knight made a growly sound as his palms swept up Lake's back, and he ravished Lake's mouth.

God, Lake took it back. His kisses weren't sweet. They were torturously sinful and infuriatingly addictive. Lake would have a hard time not using them as a measure for all future kisses.

Nobody had kissed him like this before. Confident and careful and completely absorbed in him.

Lake could drown in it.

He squeezed Knight's elbows and slunk off his lap, combing his fingers down Knight's arms to his pinkies. He hooked them. "Let's move over there."

Lake led him to the spot under the apple tree.

Knight hummed. "I could point out more cushiony places for this. Why here?"

"Just because." Lake popped the button of his shorts and shimmied out of them, along with his underwear.

Thumbs hooked into his waistband, Knight froze, gloriously sexy in the bluish yard. "Just because?"

Lake's hard cock jutted wantonly towards Knight, and heat rushed to his neck. "Uh huh. Take off your pants."

Knight stepped against him, a firm hand carefully positioning his throbbing cock against Knight's lower stomach, and then both hands fanned over his shoulders. "This is the precise spot where you charged over to check in on me and Josh."

"I wasn't checking in. I was dropping by to say hey."

"With murderous green eyes."

"Murderous!" Lake's laugh echoed in his ears. "No, I loved seeing you and Josh hitting it off. He's not forbidden."

"You need to get over the forbidden thing." Knight stepped back and shoved his pants off in an insanely suave, sexy move.

"Yes. Well." Lake glared. "I understand why it's so tempting."

Knight hummed and slotted their warm bodies together. Thigh to thigh, chest to chest, cock to aching cock. Arms circled firmly around Lake, thumb stroking his shoulder blade lightly, and Knight whispered, "You think this feels so good just because it's slightly off-limits?"

A thunderous jolt of fear bowled into Lake and he nodded emphatically. "Any other reason would freak me out. I'm sticking to this being the lure of the forbidden, if that's okay by you."

Another nip to his ear. "For now."

Lake chuckled; he couldn't help it. It grabbed hold of that fear and turned it to fizz.

Knight pulled his head back, smiling. His dark eyes crinkled. Mesmerizing. "Your laugh is infectious, Lake."

Lake flushed. "Good. The world needs more of it."

"It lights up your face." Knight swept a thumb over the bottom of his lip. "Beautiful."

"On a scale from hideous to excessively handsome, where is

beautiful? More importantly, is "good looking" before or after it?"

"What are you talking about?"

"Just wondering."

Knight read him, and Lake darted his eyes innocently away.

"You overheard me call Josh good looking. That's what this is about."

"Beautiful sounds like it should go after good looking, but the way you flirted with Josh tonight made me wonder if you think differently."

"You're quite something, Lake."

"Quite ridiculous is what I am. But . . . Josh? Really? Do you have to crush on my sort-of neighborhood nemesis?"

A disbelieving laugh. "He's not the one whose cock is rubbing tortuously against mine."

Lake pouted. "He would be, if you'd asked—"

A laughing kiss cut him off as Knight steered him back over the lawn, and somehow Lake was lowered onto the cushiony grass, refreshingly cool against his back, Knight wonderfully heavy atop him. Lake clutched him at the waist, pulling him in, as if he could consume him. Every inch of him rubbed against Knight and it still wasn't enough. Kisses roamed over his jaw, under his ear, and suctioned onto Lake's neck. He squirmed, angling for more.

"Jesus. God." A fireworks display was going on inside Lake's body, slowly working toward the grand finale. "I didn't think dads could be so good at this—oh, hell, do that again."

Knight tweaked his nipple, smiling. "Less of the dad talk please."

"Right, yes. But my point stands. I can't believe old men—"

Knight crushed him into another mind-blowing kiss, gyrating against him, making his toes curl into blades of grass.

"I can't believe mature men—"

"Nope."

"Wise?"

Knight covered his mouth with his palm, eyes dancing. "I love your babbling, but if we could reject words referring to my age, that'd be great."

He swiveled his hips, and Lake moaned against those large fingers, their gazes holding. Nervous fear re-emerged, quickly suppressed as he thrust with delicious friction and Knight released his mouth, groaning. The sound shivered through Lake; frantically, he clawed Knight nearer, biting and licking his neck, moaning other words—definitely not related to age.

So good. Highs like this should be illegal. Where have you been all my life?

Knight pushed up, straddling his thighs, eyes unsettlingly soft as they soaked him in from face to straining cock. Lake shivered, exposed, but safe. Desired.

Heart ramping, Lake captured the slow smile forming on Knight's lips. "Never stop touching me."

Knight moaned against his mouth, toppling with him to the ground. He ripped up a handful of grass and feathered the blades down his arm, over his hip, lingering where their crotches met. The ticklish sensation combined with heavier friction and Lake squirmed.

"Oh, God, you're ruining me for anyone else—"

Knight thrust his tongue into his mouth at the tail end of that, turning his words to moans. Lake wanted Knight breaching him, fucking him hard and fast, soft and slow. Pounding into him until his nerve endings combusted. "Grab that condom you carry around and get in me already."

"Nothing I'd rather do." Knight rocked against him.

"I hear a but."

"I don't have one on me. I didn't expect—"

Lake threw his arms wide in exasperation, fanning through the grass. "This might be the first time you've let me down."

"Lake." Condescendingly.

"What? You were meant to snap open an aloe vera leaf for lube and fuck me silly."

"I may not need to fuck you for that."

Lake laughed and groaned.

Knight slunk down his torso, kissing a slow trail over Lake's smooth chest and flat stomach. "Here's my proposal. We can go inside to my room and I can fuck you sillier there. Or, we could do other things here."

Knight's chin bobbed against the head of Lake's cock and Lake hissed, wanting more. Needing it. Pretty urgently. But it'd been so long since he'd been properly fucked and he didn't know when he'd have another opportunity—especially in such capable hands.

"How about half a minute here, and then we shuffle off upstairs and resume there?"

"Your smile is cocky right now."

"It's a fantastic concession."

"Concession? Hardly. That's having the cake and eating it too."

"Your smile is crooked, you horny gentleman."

Knight crawled up him and reached behind Lake's head, his hard cock on full display, proud and strong. Not quite so gentlemanly after all.

Lake approved.

He rose up on his forearms and flicked his tongue over the salty head. Knight snapped something and moaned, and Lake did it again, licked his lips, and whispered against him. "What are you doing?"

Knight pressed forward against his lips, and Lake opened. The slide of him, warm, hard, silky over his tongue, had Lake sucking eagerly, eliciting a very un-Knightly curse. "I liked your idea with the aloe vera."

Knight withdrew, a scandalous *pop* between them.

He slid back down Lake's body, gripping a serrated leaf, stopping for a slow kiss.

"My idea with—*oh*. Yes, please."

Knight peppered kisses down his chest, stomach, hip. He cupped Lake's upper thigh with practiced firmness, urging his legs apart. Knight slid between his knees and Lake's heart pounded.

Dewy, cool liquid dribbled over his inner thigh and Knight lowered his mouth, smiling. Soft and happy and almost disbelieving. Lake whimpered a good second before Knight's lips wrapped around him and wet fingers slid over his entrance with tantalizing gentleness.

Lake shut his eyes and craned his head back, immersing himself in Knight's master ministrations. He'd never been so sensitively breached, so carefully opened, so thoroughly stimulated.

Lake was talking senselessly. Pleading. Demanding Knight, just this once, not be so damn patient.

He groaned when Knight peeled him off the grass, and he grumbled all the way inside. It should have paused the desire racing through him, should have been awkward, but Lake took the stairs with stunning tempo, insisting Knight get on with it.

Knight insisted Lake not kill Garfield in his hurry.

The memory foam and feather-down covers welcomed him, but the room was too dark to make out more than bulky shapes. Lake rolled for the bedside lamp. The golden glow startled him, but he recovered when he saw an amused smile and gorgeous muscles striding into the room.

Knight found a tiny bottle of lube and checked the use-by date on the box of condoms while Lake wriggled impatiently, alone on the bed. A beefy laugh preceded Knight's return, and twinkly eyes met his. That addictive weight bore down on him and their lips locked.

The condom wrapper crinkled above his head, and Knight sat back on his haunches, rolling the latex on, adding more lube to his length.

Nervousness met neediness and, for a brief moment, Lake trembled.

"Are you okay?"

Of course Knight read him like a book.

Lake raised his chin. "Why wouldn't I be?"

Knight settled himself over Lake like a warm blanket, lube-ready cock pressed wetly against his. A feathery kiss landed on the edge of his lips. "Talk to me."

"It's nothing." At Knight's stern look, Lake rolled his eyes. "Fine. I just got . . . shy. Not something I'm particularly used to in bed." Awkwardness, absolutely, but not raw nervousness.

Knight cupped his face. "Not something I'm used to either." He whispered, "Yet I find myself feeling the same."

Oh.

Lake wound his arms loosely around Knight's shoulders and pulled himself up into a kiss. It started soft, a quiet message of reassurance.

Lake murmured against Knight's lips. "It's okay. We can be shy together."

He shuffled under Knight, parting his legs, until the tip of Knight's sheathed cock prodded his slippery entrance. Knight's breath hitched as he pressed forward.

Lake whimpered against Knight's chin and tightened his grip on his shoulders.

Knight's hand wrapped around his cock, stroking him firmly through the burn as he sank deeply into him. A year was a long time.

He clenched around Knight, adjusting to his girth, and

Knight groaned, gaze flickering fiery. Confidence returned at that look, and Lake tilted his hips, daring Knight for more.

Knight rocked into him gently, one palm rolling against his ass cheek.

Lake groaned at the friction inside, and his toes curled. He was falling from a great height, gravity racing through him. He chased after more, lifting to meet Knight's wildly growing thrusts.

Tongues met as Knight drove into him with growing need, the headboard banged against the wall, and Lake babbled pleas and curses.

He rolled Knight onto his back and sank deeper onto him, dropped his head back, body molding into each thrust. They moved so easily together, taking control and giving it seamlessly, like they'd done this a thousand times.

Skin slapped and Lake breathed in the muskiness of their sex.

Pleasure mounted.

Knight filled him with a deep grunt and pushed himself into a sitting position. Lake looped his legs around his waist, cock rubbing against Knight's stomach, adding to the blazing ache.

"Close," Lake murmured, and Knight crushed him into a kiss as he surged into him. Lake gripped his cock and jerked, moaning into Knight's hot mouth as he came. He clenched around Knight as his orgasm wrenched through him, spilling over his hand and Knight. *God.*

Knight groaned, pulsing deep inside Lake, and Lake held him through the waves.

Ragged breaths passed between them.

Dizzy, Lake chuckled and pressed an exhausted kiss on the bridge of Knight's nose. He'd never felt so spectacularly fucked before, so wonderfully sated. "That was the best sex of my life."

Knight looked flushed. "I'm quite speechless myself."

Reluctantly, Lake pulled off Knight, and they shuffled into the bathroom to clean up. "I want to crawl back into bed and sleep."

Grumpily, Lake followed Knight's lead and brushed his teeth.

They took turns spitting in the sink and Lake eyed Knight's glowing face in the mirror.

"Should I be apologizing? For baiting you into this?"

Knight met his reflection, surprise turning into cool calm. "No, Lake. I wanted seducing as much as you wanted to seduce me."

"It got the better of me." He spat again, avoiding Knight's gaze. "But now that it's out of my system, I won't do it again."

Knight focused on rinsing his toothbrush. "It's out of your system?"

"Completely."

"Just like that?"

"Uh huh. Promise."

Knight side-eyed him for a long beat. "Okay." He nodded. "We'll never do that again."

Disappointment flurried in his chest at Knight's easy acceptance, and Lake slicked on a smile. "Glad we're on the same page. But, again, for the record. Wow."

They stared at each other, still magnetized, and Lake ripped himself toward his bedroom. "Sleep well."

"Lake. . ."

He whirled around again, bouncing on the balls of his feet. "Yep?"

"It comes before beautiful."

"Huh?"

"The Josh thing. Cameron was watching Josh, sighing, and I asked him what that was about. He said he thought Josh was the hottest guy he'd met. I don't think he meant to say it aloud, and not to make a big deal, I casually agreed that Josh is good looking."

"He *is* good looking."

"That is true."

Lake met Knight's eyes before hurriedly glancing away again. "Um, okay."

Knight inclined his head and swept toward his bedroom. "Sleep well, Lake."

20

Lake slept so deeply, he didn't have the proper time to process the night before. His nerves were a grenade as he trod downstairs after a hurried shower. Their tryst was a one-time thing, and Lake wouldn't dwell on getting swept up in a passionate moment if it wasn't Knight who he'd gotten swept up with.

This could not be treated like a mistake. This was no laughing matter.

One-time it may be. But it had been special. Tender and real and wild and mind-blowing. Something Lake would cherish for a long time.

He fanned the edges of his forest-green polo shirt, sank his hands into his pockets, and entered the coffee-scented kitchen.

Wearing that soft shirt Lake loved and dark shorts, Knight was pulling vinegar from the cupboard. His bare feet had Lake sense-remembering the press and drag of his toes against Knight's.

A little sound escaped him, and Knight turned around and smiled. "Morning. Coffee's good to go." Knight sidled to the stove top as he would any other morning. "Eggs? I'm poaching them."

How could he be so normal? Seriously, not even a flicker of a blush? Had he lost all memory of their intimates connecting?

Lake filled a mug of coffee and narrowed his eyes. "How much did you drink last night?"

Knight eyed him calmly and stirred his pot of water. "A couple of beers."

"Did you hit your head?"

A soft chuckle. "Are you feeling okay?"

Lake spoke into a sip of coffee. "Of course."

"You're acting strange."

"Yes, I am. You are not."

Harry skated into the kitchen in his socks, toppling against Lake. He righted himself and winced as if the sudden movement had jolted his brain. "Some party."

"You can say that again," Lake murmured, peeking at Knight, who was cracking an egg into his pot.

Lake buried a frown in a gulp of coffee and focused on Harry, who massaged his temples. Had the news about Philip gotten to him? Or had he taken to drinking for some other reason?

Harry grabbed some coffee and took a relieved sip. "So this *thing* happened last night."

"Thing?" Another darting—and unfruitful—look to Knight.

Harry nodded. "Uh huh. With Martin. He wanted to talk to me about the nature of my karaoke choices. They were all goodbye songs. To make a clean cut—romantically. So I can focus on him as a cousin. And a friend. Anyway, I said I had lines to practice for my audition today and ran inside. But Martin followed me, said he didn't want to push, but that he'd like to understand. I completely freaked out and asked him to help me practice lines—and he did, Lake. Without any complaint. Just picked up the script and started. I could barely remember my lines I was so out of sorts. Like, it was awkward, you know? After the songs? But also, he was so helpful, and I couldn't help but feel happy he was there. God. After the first refill, I insisted on at least making it fun for him. The pitcher of margaritas probably wasn't the smartest idea. Especially since it was only me who drank it."

Harry's freckled cheeks darkened with a blush. "I don't

remember too much after that. Only laughing really hard, and later, Martin rubbing my back while I threw up in the bathroom. He cleaned up and helped me into bed, and now I'm super embarrassed."

Lake met Knight's gaze. "A very normal feeling after sharing an intense moment together."

Knight's brows lifted; he scooped his egg onto buttered toast, and passed it to Lake.

Their gazes held.

"Sure," Harry said, breaking the moment. "But how am I supposed to talk to him again?"

"I don't know."

"With honesty and frankness," Knight said, and cracked another egg into his pot.

Lake nodded slowly and tried to focus on Harry, but his gaze kept straying to Knight. "I agree. If I were you, I would say how much you loved spending last night with him, that you promise those . . . weaker moments won't happen again, and that his friendship means everything to you."

Knight cocked his head. "I must change my answer. I'd suggest taking time to look into your feelings before confronting Martin with honesty and frankness."

Lake frowned. As if he needed to look into his feelings—they were blazing through his cheeks the entire morning! "Fine," Lake gritted out. "Do that. Take a week before you talk to him about it again."

Harry nodded profusely. "Absolutely. You're right."

"Did you talk to Cameron last night?" Lake asked, salivating over his delicious-looking poached egg on toast.

"Barely. Why? Is he holding auditions?"

"Not yet." Ugh. Lake had to tell him Philip met someone. Their circles were too close, and he'd rather arm Harry with the information so he wasn't unexpectedly punched in the face with it.

Lake set his coffee down next to his toast. "Come upstairs with me."

Harry and Knight looked at him curiously.

"What?" Lake mouthed to Knight. "Harry and I need to flip mattresses . . ."

THE WORK-WEEK DRAGGED. AT LEAST, THE HOURS IN THE office did. As soon as he returned home, he settled into a routine with Knight, organizing Cameron's Ask Austen surprise party, fighting over the remote, and pretending to read in his company until Knight rolled his eyes, took the book from him, and read aloud. He sure was making headway through *Moby Dick*.

On Thursday, an offer came in for his cottage, and on Friday afternoon—stealing away early from work—Knight and the agent they'd hired agreed that Lake should accept the offer.

Of course, they still had to finalize it, but he was finally selling. His childhood home wouldn't be his anymore. He paced before the fireplace in front of Knight, who spent more time watching him than reading the Kindle sitting on his lap.

"Are you having second thoughts?" Knight murmured.

"No. Absolutely not." Lake's sock squealed as he marched the length of the room.

Knight gave up the pretense of reading and set his Kindle down. He clasped his hands between parted thighs. "Something's going on."

ANYTA SUNDAY

"I couldn't stand being in the cottage."

"And yet?"

Lake halted and his voice came out strangled, "Why does it feel so hard to say goodbye?"

Knight strode swiftly to the hearth and wrapped comforting arms around him. Lake buckled immediately, forehead resting at the intersection of Knight's neck and shoulder. He breathed him in, and sighed. "You smell clean and woodsy and so together."

Knight squeezed him warmly.

Lake sniffed. "Thank you for being here."

"Do you want to drive over there? Say goodbye properly?"

"Was that a suggestion? Or are you offering to come with me?"

Knight kissed the top of his head. "I'll drive."

He made to untangle them, and Lake protested. "Just one more minute."

Saying goodbye was cathartic and exactly what Lake needed. He led Knight around the property, telling him all the stories he could remember. The happiness, the cheekiness, the sorrow. The tree he'd climbed to spy on the boy next door, where he realized he was gay. The rooftop he'd fallen from and broken his nine-year-old arm. His bedroom where he'd slept under glow-in-the-dark stars.

When Lake was exhausted, Knight drove them home and insisted he rest, while he visited Taylor.

A nap revived Lake, and when he woke, he swatted the grogginess from his eyes, picked up his phone and keys, and headed to Taylor's.

The late afternoon was sunny without a cloud in the sky. The scent of burning charcoal carried on soft breezes. A cat raced across the road. Most people knew one another here—at least by sight—and Lake loved it. Particularly how short the walk to his best friend's place was.

158

Taylor was bent over the trunk of his car, and he greeted him with a swat to his ass.

Taylor turned around—

"Oh, shit. You're not Taylor."

The man before him had a similar athletic build, but he had a tattoo of a rose at his throat that disappeared under his collar, and he sported a three-day beard. His bright eyes were humorous and currently laughing at him. Lake recognized the guy from pictures over the last few weeks.

West reached out a hand. "You must be Lake."

Lake shook it. "What gave me away?"

"Green-eyed and gorgeous—and you fit the bill."

That was coming on a little strong, but that smile—cheekily playful, wasn't it?

Lake dropped his hand and laughed. "A green-eyed, gorgeous groper, apparently."

"No harm, no foul." West hauled a duffel bag out of the trunk and slung it over his shoulder.

Curious. "Planning on staying awhile?"

"Just the weekend," West said, shutting the trunk, "while I'm sorting out some . . . things."

They headed inside to Taylor and Amy setting up their telescope wedding gift, and Knight reading a newspaper and sipping tea.

"I love how at home everyone is here," West murmured. "I'll just drop this into the room."

He hiked toward the guest room. He was a good-looking guy. Nice height, warm and easygoing.

Lake should probably like him.

Knight glanced up from the business section, surprised. "Lake. I thought you were resting."

His shirt, now unbuttoned, revealed a turquoise T-shirt underneath, and the lighting flowed over him, illuminating threads of gold in his hair and eyes. He was laughter and hugs ready-and-waiting. Lake folded himself into an adjacent chair. "I rested, and now I'm here."

"If you'd move your elbows . . ." Lake drew them off the newspaper, and Knight turned the page.

Lake took a section of the paper; the tingly feeling at his cheek told him Knight was studying his profile. Air stirred as Knight leaned in. "Lake, what are you doing?"

"Reading an article."

"It's the Classifieds."

"Best part. Are you interested in a tall, gently-muscled man, who can appreciate a garden and has a good sense of humor? Because you have competition."

"I'm interested in the way you keep glancing at the career-opportunities column."

Noticed that, did he? "Now the house is sold, I have to start fixing the rest of my life."

"Read on."

Two job descriptions later, West returned, now wearing a neat Henley; the stem of his rose tattoo stretched to his chest. Armored with chocolates and a gift for Taylor and Amy, he thanked them again for letting him crash there for the weekend.

Lake watched the bearded man intently.

Was this really the same man who'd failed to show up for Taylor? His parents must have pressured him tremendously not to socialize with Taylor's family. He seemed too sincere for anything less. He leaned toward Knight and lowered his voice.

"You were a little harsh about him."

Knight's gaze laser-focused on West. "Is that right?" he bit off.

"I mean, look how thoughtful he is."

Knight made a non-committal sound in his throat and returned to his newspaper. Perhaps he was reflecting? Realizing he'd been hasty in his judgment?

West slung himself opposite Lake, on Knight's other side. "What are you two up to?"

Knight answered curtly, "Reading."

Lake stifled his amusement. Not quite over his prejudice, then. "Knight's a reader. He's encouraging me to pick up a few books too."

West grinned. "What books?"

"The old ones."

"Classics," Knight murmured.

"Exactly, those. I'm most of the way through *Moby Dick*."

West's brows shot up. "What do you think?"

"The title is misleading." West blinked, Knight cleared his throat, and Lake continued, "I know more about whales than I ever thought I would."

"Want a confession?" West said playfully, and Lake leaned in to hear more. "At school I only read the Cliff's notes."

"You absolute rebel."

"A prerequisite to join the club."

Knight's phone beeped. He checked it and smiled. "Josh."

"Josh?" A flicker of pleasant surprise crossed West's face.

Lake queried, "Do you remember him?"

"We bumped into each other a fair bit. Friendly guy. Smart."

Knight looked up from his phone. "He's inviting us to his place for cake."

Lake's chair screeched as he hurried to pull out his phone.

He *was* invited this time.

Taylor called from behind the couch, waving his phone around. "West, you too. Josh said anyone can tag along."

Lake stared at his invite. Did he want to go? What if Josh spent the whole afternoon flirting with Knight?

"So, we're all off to Josh's, then?" West asked, looking eager.

Lake sighed. "I suppose I'll come."

"Of course you'll come," Knight said. "There's cake."

Lake stood reluctantly. "I'll be needing a lot of it."

21

L ake kept stride alongside an eager West the entire way to Josh's, jumping from subject to subject, and it was eerie how well they meshed for having only just met.

West didn't seem as fickle or flighty as Knight had suggested. He seemed genuine, kind, and level-headed.

Until he started using his camera as a mirror outside Josh's place, fussing with his hair and asking if anyone had Chap-Stick. "Two top buttons open, or just one?"

Lake—put off by the sudden display of vanity—retreated to a quietly observing Knight, vowing never to act like that himself, and if he should, would Knight please clap him over the back of the head.

"Gladly."

Lake smirked. "I'd offer the same, but I've rarely seen you indulge in your looks. You're naturally attractive, so I guess you don't need to fuss. Not that I can imagine you fussing regardless. You don't care about what anyone thinks."

"Is that right?"

"I like that you don't try hard. That you're okay being one of the less handsome people in a room."

"I hardly know what to say."

"You're welcome."

Josh's parents greeted them at the door on their way out, motioning them into the house, and they moved into the large polished-marble kitchen. A dozen other guests gathered around the island, including Cameron, who broke away and made for Lake and Knight. "Quite the cake, isn't it?" Cameron whispered.

Perched on an elegant stand was a three-tiered wedding cake with frosted roses and real strawberries. Atop, two male figures embraced.

Cameron sighed. "It arrived this afternoon. No note or mention who it was from, just instructions to deliver to Josh. He was shocked."

Someone knocked a plate of cake off the table and icing mushed against the tiled floor. Cameron's lips flattened. "That was my bit. Shouldn't have left it so close to the edge."

Disheartened, he slumped off to clean it.

Lake should probably help him, but that would inevitably lead to talking about their days. He could handle hearing about Cameron's awesome, productive, world-changing day at the office, but not on the heels of selling his cottage. Still raw from the afternoon, he might be triggered by anything.

"I'll go," Knight murmured.

Lake watched him walk over, grateful and touched by his unwavering kindness.

His eye caught on West lounging—a little uncertainly—in the doorway.

Lake sagged against the other side of the frame. "So. Big cake, huh?"

"Huge. I heard it was a gift."

"Pretty romantic one."

"Yes."

"I wonder who sent it to him. Whoever they are, they're clearly from around here. That cake has *Cody's Bakery* written all over it, and *Cody's* hasn't set up an online presence yet."

"You sound like that would be odd."

Lake shrugged. "Josh hasn't been back long. If I wasn't so sure that was a *Cody's* cake, I'd have thought it was from a secret admirer from England."

"Hmm, perhaps he met someone recently?"

Lake frowned, glancing at their handsome, happy host serving cake to his friends. "Someone he just met sending him a wedding cake would be weird. He seems too at ease for that. I suspect he knows exactly who sent it." Lake swallowed. "Someone he knows well, that lives around here."

Lake's gaze panned over the crowd to Knight and Cameron holding paper plates of cake. Each layer of the gift had been cut into, the top a succulent-looking chocolate, the middle, densely pink with berries, and the bottom a more modest vanilla. "I'm grabbing myself a piece. Want one?"

West shook his head. "I'm good admiring the view, thank you."

Lake zigzagged through guests to Josh, who gazed at the figures atop his gift, gnawing his lip. "Quite the gesture," Lake opened, hoping Josh would supply more information.

Josh nodded, Adam's apple jutting with a big swallow.

"You must wonder who sent it to you."

Josh merely shook his head. "Want a piece?"

"Chocolate, please."

Cake in hand, Lake watched Josh retreat to the large bay window. Was he overwhelmed by the attention? He kept looking back at them with a mixture of pleasure and apprehension.

Lake settled into a two-person armchair with a view of Josh and the party bubbling around the kitchen. Across from him, Knight and Cameron conversed near a wonderfully large bookshelf. Look at Knight there, surrounded by books. Right at home.

He texted Harry to join them at Josh's. West plonked down next to him. "Much nicer here."

Lake flushed and lifted his plate of cake to take a bite. Rich. Succulent.

Did West like him? Did he like West back?

"If you're staying at Taylor's the whole weekend, you should come to the party Knight and I are hosting tomorrow."

"Sounds great. Will a lot of your friends be there?" West asked, scanning the room. "I wouldn't want to crash anything special."

"Pretty much everyone in this room and Cameron's colleagues. Keep it quiet, though. Cameron has no idea. Surprise party."

West smiled widely. "I am a fan of surprises."

Lake told him about the Ask Austen theme, and promised to send him a character profile later. "You keep looking at Josh. Everything okay?"

"Yes, absolutely," West said, nodding ardently. "Only wondering why he's sitting alone in this room full of people. I hope he's feeling okay." A light laugh. "Lay off the cake. It might be dodgy."

"One of *Cody's*? Never."

West stood. "You know what, maybe I'll go ask. Let's see if he recognizes me."

Lake watched him catch Josh's attention. A pity he couldn't see Josh's face and gauge his reaction to West in his house. Josh would take the tag-along guest with grace. Of course—he'd texted as much.

A hand ruffled the back of his hair, and Taylor rounded the couch and dropped into it. His hair stuck out at odd angles and a thread of grass revealed what he'd been up to the last ten minutes with Amy.

"You really left your friend to fend for himself," Lake chastised.

Taylor heated. "Sorry. West is good at mingling."

"I can see that."

Taylor inclined his head toward Knight. "Dad's really invested in that period drama business venture."

"He's invested in Cameron." Chatting to him, making sure

he was feeling all right, always ready to listen . . . "No one is as good and kind and thoughtful as your dad."

Taylor laughed. "Got any more adjectives there, Lake?"

"Good-natured. Considerate. Loving."

"Don't forget romantic," Taylor added, mischievously.

Lake's heart thumped, and it took him three tries to stab cake onto his fork. "Romantic?"

Taylor shuffled closer, his voice low and excited. "Hear me out. I've been wondering this since Karaoke last week, and the more I think about it, the more it makes sense."

Lake swallowed the nervous lump in his throat. "What makes sense?"

"I think my dad is into Josh."

Lake's stomach dropped to his feet. His laugh tasted like ash. "Knight and Josh?"

"Yeah, wouldn't that be great?"

"Josh is our age. Wouldn't that be, like, weird for you?"

Taylor shrugged. "Dad hangs around you and Cameron all the time, I'm used to seeing him with guys our age and . . . I don't know. Maybe a little weird, but relationships evolve."

Exactly what Knight had said. He'd been convinced Taylor would understand how much time he and Lake had been spending together. Turns out he was right.

But Knight and Josh?

"I'm surprised you think they could be a thing."

"I'm not saying they are. Yet. But they get along well from what I can tell."

Knight, with painfully pointed timing, glanced past Cameron toward Josh and West framed in the bay window. Words stuck in his throat, "You think your dad should go for it?"

Taylor leaned an arm casually on Lake's shoulder, but it added to the weight sinking his stomach. "Whatever makes Dad happy."

Anxiety lanced through Lake. "Lots of things make him happy, not only Josh!"

Taylor frowned.

One long deep breath, and Lake calmed himself. Mostly. "I mean, he loves his garden and reading and has a routine he seems good with. Does he really need romance?"

"What's gotten into you, Lake? You're usually dying to play matchmaker about now."

"I'm not feeling Knight and Josh together. Knight deserves only the deepest, truest love, and I'd hate to see him settle."

"Maybe if you weren't so envious of Josh, you'd see it. They're both smart, accomplished, kind, gay men."

Josh laughed at something West said and dammit, he was clearly an attractive man. And far cleverer than Lake could ever be.

Knight had agreed that Josh made a better match than Paul, too.

Maybe Lake's encouragement had helped Knight see Josh as a possibility? Maybe Knight had been slowly falling for Josh all along? Maybe Knight's sexy tryst with Lake had been a little something to take the edge off. Had Knight been imagining he was Josh the whole time? Was that why it'd felt so raw and tender and real? Had he been extrapolating his feelings for Josh while rocking Lake's sexual world?

A painful consideration.

Because . . . because he hated how superior Josh was.

Maybe if Lake followed through with things more? If he actually studied hard enough to call himself a photographer, or a cook. If he actually read more of the books he said he would . . .

"Dad is such a family man," Taylor continued. "I want him to have that again."

Lake cricked his neck whipping to look at Taylor so fast. "You think he'll want kids again?"

"He's not so old. He might."

"Not with Josh!"

"With whoever he falls in love with."

"If he wants kids, I'm sure you and Amy won't wait forever. He'll be there for yours. We'll babysit them whenever you and Amy need a break."

Taylor's brows hopped. "Planning on renting a room with dad for a while?" He leaned close, chuckling. "Maybe you should chat more with West."

"I don't want to talk about romance anymore. I'd rather talk to Cameron about how many subscribers he has."

"Ouch, bit of an attitude there, Lake." Taylor slapped his thigh. "Another clue. Dad said he'd never had such a fascinating conversation as he had with Josh."

Lake stared at the cake on his lap. It hurt to swallow. "Really?"

"Yeah. Good conversation makes for good partnership. Speaking of which," he said, checking his phone, "Amy wants to chat with me about something . . ."

Taylor's eyes glittered and he leaped to his feet. "You'll be okay?"

Lake waved him off. "Insatiable."

"Wait until you find Mr. Right. It's even better when you're in love."

Taylor left, and Lake picked at cake crumbs.

Across the room, Knight laughed at something Cameron said, and the warm, hearty sound of it dug deep in Lake's gut.

If Knight and Josh started something, Josh would be at Knight's all the time. Living there would become awkward, and Lake would have to give up the only other place he'd thought of as home . . .

No, Knight couldn't fall for Josh.

Cameron received a call and excused himself, and Knight

picked up his plate of half-eaten strawberry cake and sat next to Lake.

A weird gurgle escaped and he fought down an explosion of anxious shivers. Almost successfully. The cushions shifted under them as Knight made himself comfortable, lounging into the couch, one arm stretched along the back, disappearing behind Lake.

Vibrations of Knight's nearness caressed his shoulder blades. He shoved another forkful of cake into his mouth.

"What do you think of the cake?" Knight asked.

"How it tastes? Or as a romantic gesture?"

"How it tastes. I assume you approve of it as a gesture, being the romantic you are."

Oh, God. Had Knight sent the wedding cake as a quiet declaration? Was he nervously awaiting Josh's response?

"It's a wedding cake. Whoever sent it must feel confident Josh returns their feelings."

"I hope the feelings are mutual. I see you have a chocolate piece. Any good?"

Lake swapped their plates. "It'd taste better if there wasn't such a mystery around it. Oh, the strawberry is delicious."

Knight chuckled, the corners of his dark eyes pinching.

"What?"

"Nothing."

"You're thinking something."

Another laugh. "I confess, I haven't shaken your earlier words about me being one of the less handsome people in the room. It's made me unusually self-conscious."

"Why on Earth?" Bewilderment pinched Lake's brow. "For the record, you are *not* one of the less handsome people in this room. I just like that you would be okay if you were. You're confident enough to know that you're the most attractive." Lake used his fork to lightly prod Knight's forehead, followed by his chest. "Here and here is what matters, and you have all that in abundance."

Lake went back to eating Knight's cake. Delicious, even though his nerves were shot.

How did he ask Knight if he'd sent it? How did he not get upset that Knight never asked his opinion? Lake thought they were open to sharing everything with one another.

Or maybe that had just been Lake.

"Taylor said that you and Josh have been having fascinating conversations."

Knight slowly inclined his head. "We have."

"About what?"

"The economics of saving the Amazon."

"I thought Jeff Bezos was a billionaire?"

"The Amazon. Not Amazon."

Ah, crap. "What are the economics of saving the rainforest?"

Knight delved into an economic summary, and it was far more interesting than Lake wanted it to be. These were the kinds of conversations Knight and Josh had? Help.

"Yeah, cattle raising is a bad tradeoff. But the people need money to live. Can't the rest of the world pay them not to destroy it?"

Knight smiled. "Interesting, isn't it?"

Lake sighed. Yeah, it was.

Knight shifted and spoke at his ear, words stroking his lobe. "Are you okay?"

"Yep. Totally okay. I love that you have these conversations with others."

"Me too."

"You should make a habit of discussing these worldly conundrums."

"I do."

"And after you've had another fascinating conversation

with Josh, you should tell me all about it, so I can share in the delight."

"I like your newfound interest."

"You can talk to him every day about economics and morals, and I promise I'll encourage you. So when you go to bed and reflect on the most memorable parts of the day, maybe you'll think of me too, and how much I want you having these *fascinating* conversations."

Knight hummed thoughtfully and then gestured toward Josh and West. "They're beckoning us over."

Josh sat smiling quietly on the windowsill, and West waved to join them.

Despite West's charmingly crooked grin, Lake's gaze stuck to Knight the entire way.

22

The next morning, Lake regretted the inferiority of his stargazing. After cake, the entire party had walked to Taylor's to use his telescope and check out the night sky. Halfway into the impromptu starry party, Lake began grieving his laziness and wishing he'd paid more attention when his dad had tried to teach him all the constellations.

Quite the fool he was.

So intent on being interesting, he'd elaborated a few things.

Who knew Josh would be an expert in this area as well? His gently humored way of correcting Lake's misinformation had Lake's stomach in painful, mortified knots.

Lake groaned, and thumped his head against the overhead cupboards.

At least he could follow a recipe for banana muffins. The delicious scent wafted from the oven and hopefully lured Knight downstairs. And then what? Convince Knight he had good qualities? Weasel out information on whether Knight had sent that cake?

Fuuuuck.

Footsteps came down the hall and Lake whisked around to—

Harry flopped into a chair at the dining table. "Such an interesting night last night." Harry's smile wobbled. "I wish I knew as much about stars as you and Josh do."

Lake groaned. "Don't compare us, Harry. I know the equivalent of one solar system to his galactic knowledge."

"You explained it better, though. I preferred your fun facts to Josh's rote statistics."

"Fun facts that were mostly discredited. You're being nice, but Josh really knew his stars."

"Well I enjoyed your enthusiasm, and I overheard West saying the fun-fact part was his favorite."

"He probably meant watching me get taken down a peg."

Harry tried protesting again, but Lake cut him off, slinging himself into the chair beside him. "What's the matter? Are you on the verge of bawling?"

Harry set his phone on the table, taking a long, shaky breath. "I was stupid. On the way to bed last night, I texted Martin. Just to see how he was." He swatted his eyes. "Turns out he was on a date."

Oh. "I'm so sorry, Harry."

Harry nodded, eyes watering. "Ugh, this is stupid. It was completely over. It is. It's something to get used to."

"The more I try to understand love, the less I seem to know. It's a big knife playing Operation with your heart."

"Can we, I don't know, get out of here for the morning?"

Lake turned off the oven—muffins looked done—and grabbed his keys. Harry needed a distraction, and Lake could enjoy some distraction too. "Let's go."

"How about instead of coffee at Tranquil we go to *Cody's*?" Lake asked Harry, aiming for the artisan bakery tucked between a barber shop and a violin restoration store.

Exquisite baked goods greeted them in colorful rows, and the richness of melted chocolate filled Lake's nose.

Lake grinned at the cute Māori guy behind the counter. "It must be frustrating for customers."

The baker—presumably Cody?—snapped his head up. "Hmm? Frustrating?"

"There are so many amazing cakes here, how does anyone ever choose?"

Cody grinned, two big dimples popping his cheeks. "Can I get you something?"

"Two coffees." Lake drummed his fingers over the wooden counter. "Also, I was wondering about that impressive three-tiered cake you delivered yesterday."

"I delivered more than one impressive three-tiered cake."

"The one with the two male figures embracing on the top."

"Ah. Good, wasn't it?"

Truth. "Best thing I've tasted. Tell me, do you know who sent it?"

"Couldn't tell you if I did."

"It was a guy right? Was his voice like warm honeyed whiskey? Did he sound pretentious? Like he might always be right?"

Cody smiled and shook his head in amusement. "Sorry, can't say."

Lake grumbled but paid for their drinks and let Cody get back to work. "Let's find a seat—"

Lake almost dropped his coffee. Seated at the window was none other than Josh.

Josh watched Lake and Harry with a half-smile. Possibly a grimace.

Slipping into some glee, Lake joined Josh at his table. "We didn't see you there."

Harry sat next to Lake on the grainy oak bench.

Josh pinned him with a knowing look. "Have fun bugging the baker for details about my surprise cake?"

Lake laughed. "What can I say? I like solving mysteries."

Instead of giving Lake the information he wanted, Josh nodded.

"Oh, look!" Harry pointed toward the sidewalk. "Isn't that West at the corner?"

Sure enough, West was sauntering in their direction holding a package under his arm.

Harry waved wildly, catching West's attention. West grinned, and ducked into the bakery.

"This is unexpected," West said, shifting his gaze fleetingly to Josh.

West's package was wrapped in brown paper and tied in string. "Out shopping?"

"Picked something up for my mother. I'm meeting her at home in a half hour."

Josh shifted on his bench, making room for him. "Join us, then."

Harry cocked his head. "I thought you were staying with Taylor?"

"I am," West said.

"But your mum lives here?"

West remained quiet for a few beats, worry lines creasing his brow. His check twitched. "Friends from her congregation are staying in the guest room. Is the coffee any good?"

"Excellent," murmured Josh, and Lake agreed.

He frowned after West as he ordered at the counter. Mention of his family had made him uncomfortable, and that lie about friends staying in the guest room was a mystery.

Too many mysteries. They made his stomach twist in knots.

One in particular. What was Knight doing right now? Had he discovered Lake's muffins and the note to help himself?

Was he, even momentarily, thinking of Lake?

"Lake?"

"Huh?" Lake dragged his focus back to Josh.

"Are you excited about the party?"

"Sure. Yes. Absolutely."

He was not thrilled Josh was coming, but maybe it was for the best. Maybe tonight a mystery would be solved.

23

"Twice in one day," Lake said as he opened Cameron's door wide. "What a pleasure."

Josh smiled. "Knight asked if I'd help him set up the marquee and dance floor?"

Damn he looked good. His remarkably blue hair had been dyed since the bakery this morning. He wore spanking new jeans that were inappropriately form-fitting for setting up a party, but that's not why he'd worn them, was it? "He might have mentioned it," Lake bit out. "He's in the garden, behind the pool."

With two hours to set up before Cameron returned—from a location-viewing on the peninsula—Lake couldn't completely begrudge the help.

"I heard Cameron's brother is coming back from Europe today," Josh said, stepping over the threshold. "You told him about the party, right?"

"Of course. I'm not an idiot."

Josh sauntered through the house, and Lake whipped off a Facebook message to Cameron's oldest brother Brandon, telling him about the party celebrating their YouTube channel successes.

He stuffed his phone into his pocket and eased the door closed.

A boot planted itself in the frame and Lake yanked the door open, revealing West and his throat tattoo and neat beard. "Taylor says I should make myself useful."

"Rich. Taylor still hasn't shown up." West rang out a jolly laugh. He seemed in better spirits than he had earlier.

Lake led him to the back garden where Josh and Knight huddled together over the marquee instructions.

"You hired a dance floor?" West said, grinning.

"We thought Cameron would like it. Besides, with the theme of the evening, at least one part of the night should be classy."

"I got your email—how will this work, exactly?"

"Drop your prescribed dilemma in conversation, and make a little act of it." Lake pulled a piece of paper from his pocket and unfolded it. "Everyone gets one of these at the door, along with a pencil. One side has all the names of the guests who are coming—some, you can see, are paired. Those are couples."

West scoured over the list. "You and Knight are a couple?"

"We're the hosts. We figured we'd do a dilemma together." Lake bit his lip. He'd been a little cheeky in what 'dilemma' he'd given them, but Knight hadn't hesitated. Not for a minute. "Anyway," Lake flipped the page around to thirty text boxes filled with Austen-styled advice, "match the best advice with the most guests and win a bottle of Lakewood Bourbon." Lake winked. "Worth over $200 a bottle now. Limited supply."

West watched Josh struggle with a marquee pole. "The bourbon sounds good. Maybe the two best scorers have to dance?" He grinned. "Or kiss. That'll spice things up."

It'd certainly make it interesting—and thankfully Lake and Knight would have to excuse themselves, since they knew the answers. They could enjoy from the sidelines with no sick worry churning in his belly at the idea of Josh and Knight locking lips . . . "Fantastic idea."

Knight helped Josh with his pole, and Lake was hit with Josh's grateful smile when his gaze darted around the garden, slowing over Lake and West.

Josh's smile deepened, rubbing in his feelings for Knight.

So much for being amiable and kind and perfect. That smile was all gloating.

Knight calmly and deftly moved on to the next bit of assembly. Casual sneakers, the shorts he'd worn retiling Lake's cottage, and the most ragged T-shirt he owned, which was barely ragged at all. Slightly faded tan that nevertheless worked with his hair and slight stubble and eyes . . .

Josh moved toward Knight, and Lake found himself jogging over. No idea what he was doing, except being a slave to his gut.

His gaze snagged on Knight's and didn't let go. "Um. West had the best idea . . ."

Knight listened patiently, gripping a pole like a staff. "Doesn't excite me, but then I won't be taking part. Not that I ever intended to dance."

Lake gaped at him. "It was your idea to get the dance floor."

"It was *your* idea, and I agreed. I'm no good at the grinding stuff."

Lake held his tongue.

"But I'll happily watch you bounce about," Knight continued.

"I hope you change your mind."

"Maybe. If there's a slow dance, and the right partner."

Josh filled Lake's peripheral vision and his stomach crunched. "Know what? Sitting out is good. It's fine. You should do that. Now," Lake curled a hand around the pole above Knight's. "Where does this go?"

CAMERON RETURNED HOME TWENTY MINUTES TOO EARLY.

Lake shoved the last box of champagne into the kitchen and ran to stop Cameron opening the door—

Voices outside on the porch.

Cameron and . . . Knight.

Knight sounded determined to hold Cameron's attention. "How was your day? I'm glad I caught you, I had a few thoughts on rebranding your channel. I wrote them down. Can you pop over for a few minutes?"

"Really? Great! Let me drop my bag inside and—"

"No! I mean," Knight cleared his throat, "you'll need your laptop to write notes."

"Duh. Of course. Excellent."

Lake sagged against the door, relieved at their retreat, and pulled out his phone.

Lake: You actually have notes? Ideas on rebranding? Or did you make that up?

Knight: I've left him in the lounge while I sort something out.

Lake: You're the hero of the hour.

Knight: Yes.

Lake grinned, earning an arched brow from West, who was busy stringing up streamers. He flopped onto the couch in the empty living room.

Lake: Make sure to pat yourself on the back.

Knight: After I do what has to be done.

Lake: What about naming it Austen Studios? It sounds professional and instantly recognizable.

Minutes later, the doorbell rang and Lake handed over the task of welcoming the guests to Taylor. Then locked himself in the bathroom.

It was ridiculous. He should be out there helping, and Knight was busy distracting Cameron, but . . . it itched in him. *Burned*. He wanted to keep chatting. About anything. Trivial or . . . not.

Lake: You know, it's almost been a week since Karaoke . . .

His finger hovered over send. He rubbed his phone against his forehead, wanting to remind Knight of the incredible passion they'd shared.

Knight: Austen Studios. Fantastic idea, Cameron loves it.

A heavy breath left him. He deleted his message. Stupid to bring up that night over text anyway.

Lake: Good. Great. The guests are arriving. Bring him over in twenty.

"I can't believe you did this," Cameron said, hours later, voice raised against Classic Hits blaring from the outdoor speaker.

Lake steered him and pineapple-shirt Harry around the back of the marquee, where he could hear them talk. "I hope you're enjoying yourself."

"I am. Love the game, too." Cameron tugged his tiny pencil from his back pocket. "You still haven't given me a clue who you and Knight are. Where is Knight, anyway?"

Lake wished he knew. Every time he spotted him, someone whisked him away into conversation. Riveting conversations, no doubt.

"He'll be around somewhere," Harry said, eyeing the dance floor longingly, like he'd been doing all evening. "Are you sure neither of you can swing dance?"

A figure slunk past them, steering for the trees at the back of the property. West?

Pencil and paper at the ready, Cameron towed Harry along to chase after a couple pinching martinis, and Lake stole after West.

West paced, speaking tightly into his phone. ". . . I told you everything you needed to know this morning. This is my life . . . No, you made the ultimatum. You have to respect my choice. I don't care what Dad has to say . . . No . . . Will you change *your* mind?" West craned his head skyward. "Fine. I'll come around tomorrow. But this is the last weekend I'm hiding like this."

Lake stood frozen halfway between the marquee and West. He'd wanted to solve a mystery, but overhearing this conversation felt wrong.

He started to turn back, but West pivoted around, startling

at the sight of him. Realization clouded West's expression. West sighed and sagged against a knotty tree trunk.

With a sympathetic smile, Lake joined him.

West ran a hand through his hair. "You probably had your suspicions already."

Lake didn't know what to say. What he'd heard had sounded serious. And saddening. "Taylor mentioned your family is conservative."

"I don't want to hide who I love . . ." West stared out toward the shimmying couples on the dancefloor and the pockets of guests laughing around the garden. "I won't. Not after tomorrow. Not once I've finally severed these ties."

West gazed at Lake. "I want to dance and kiss without fearing someone from their church will see and spurn Mum and Dad. All their friends, their whole life. I've chosen them every time, but I . . ."

He was quiet. Maybe he felt like he'd shared too much.

West sighed.

An awkward beat passed, and Lake tentatively patted his shoulder.

"You're a great guy, Lake. So easy to talk to. I'm sorry about this." West glanced away, embarrassed. "I need to take a walk. Alone. We'll catch up later."

Lake was sad to see him go. They hadn't known each other long, but West seemed genuine and kind. The type of guy Lake *should* crush on.

So why didn't he feel that happy dreaminess of a crush? Why had he no inclination to laugh and dance and be stupid? Why did he tense up every time he imagined West asking him out?

Lake wandered the party until he found Knight at the edge of the pool, dipping his legs into the water, hands braced at the edges, tips of his fingers touching the glittering surface.

Shoes toed off, Lake joined him, gasping at the flow of cold water around his calves.

"Did I see West leave?" Knight asked, watching the water.

"Yeah."

"I'm sorry, Lake. You were getting along with him."

Lake shrugged. *Not as much as Knight imagined.* "I'm sorry too. Not about West. About my behavior."

"Behavior?" Knight queried.

"The absolutely atrocious envy I have of Josh." Lake stared at their hands, an inch between them. "I know it's not been subtle."

"Subtle is never a word I've associated with you, Lake. Neither would I want it to be."

Lake glanced sideways, struck by the warmth of his tone. Heat crept up his neck. "I know you like Josh."

"Yes," Knight replied. "He's a likeable man."

Alarm and fear created a belly-twisting mixture and it took all his control to keep his voice even. "I want you happy." Lake swallowed hard. "If he makes you happy . . ." Pained, Lake continued, "Josh is smart and talented. At everything, apparently."

Color deepened the contours of Knight's cheeks and he struggled to hold Lake's gaze. A fight he nevertheless won. "You think *Josh* would make me happy?"

"I mean," Lake said, raising his hands, "I learned my lesson about matchmaking. I'm not pushing you together." He couldn't even if he wanted to. The idea alone . . . "You know what, none of this is my business. It was stupid of me to bring it up. Forget I ever said anything."

"You're wrong, Lake. Josh is a good man, but I have never —not for a minute—wanted anything more with him."

Lake blinked. "Why not?" he said, incredulously. "He's perfect!"

A chuckle. "He's subtle. Too controlled in his thoughts and

actions. I prefer a man who thrives in the moment. Who happily disagrees with me, who I can disagree with. A man one-hundred percent himself."

A jumble of nerves fired in Lake's stomach. "Oh."

Self-consciousness consumed Lake. He rubbed his nape, staring at his knees. "Knightly?"

"Emerett?"

Lake smiled softly. "I never liked the sound my first name." He met Knight's gaze. "Until you started using it."

Hopefulness flickered in Knight's eyes. His lips parted as if to speak, but his focus darted behind Lake, and a sigh funneled from him.

Cameron and Harry plunked near them, sinking their legs into the pool.

Pencil in hand, Cameron looked at Lake and Knight. "We're waiting."

Knight hummed thoughtfully and Lake palmed his thigh, fingers pulsing over cotton and skin.

He clasped Knight's shoulder and pulled him into a kiss. Their lips lingered for two long beats. A ticklish power source threaded its way deep inside, and his chest hiccupped as a warm, gently calloused hand covered his.

He turned away, lightheaded. Disoriented. Unsure how to breathe through the shivers mounting inside him.

He'd sunk into that kiss like second nature and barely thought about it.

He wanted to do it again.

Cameron and Harry blinked at them, and Lake cleared his throat. "Oh no, whatever shall I do?" Lake exclaimed, hoping his words didn't shake. "He's my best friend's father."

Laughter behind them. "You really commit to drama, Lake. Nice." Taylor squeezed between him and Knight, breaking their contact. He scanned the back of his Ask Austen sheet, searching Austen-influenced pieces of advice for their match. "Concealment, if concealment be possible, is all that remains. Or . . . I must go to my room where I am free to think and be wretched." Taylor winced. "Sounds a bit harsh. I guess it depends on the extent of your feelings—and absolutely, try to make your best friend understand." Taylor winked.

Lake shifted, kicking his feet through the water, and laughed tightly. "I'm sleeping with your dad."

"Shock. Horror." Taylor theatrically fanned a hand against his chest. "How could you?"

Lake looked to Knight. "There were . . . feelings. They overwhelmed—overwhelm—me."

Taylor tutted. "You should be ashamed of yourself."

"I'm not." Lake held Taylor's gaze. "Your dad and I have the most intimate connection I've ever experienced."

Booming laughter. "Yikes," Taylor said, "even for the game that's too much info."

Lake folded back and closed his mouth on saying more.

"Our connection means everything," Knight said quietly to Taylor, in a matter-of-fact way.

Lake's chest fluttered, ridiculously hopeful. Was he acting . . . or not?

Cameron shoved himself out of the pool, a gleeful expression on his face. "My brother's back. I gotta . . ." He charged off, water spraying over Lake's arm. "Brandon!"

Taylor snagged his dad in conversation, and Lake shuffled over to Harry, who had paled considerably. "You okay?"

Harry gulped. "I wasn't expecting Philip."

What? Lake scoured the backyard and spotted shiny alligator shoes moving toward them.

Next to Philip was the guy from Josh's party. The one Cameron worked with. Trey-someone. Lake should have anticipated this, but he'd thought Philip would never agree to come. Not after . . .

Ugh. Uncomfortable.

Poor Harry!

"He's not worth getting upset over, Harry. God, I'm so sorry for ever trying to set you up. Okay, he's coming over. Smile and nod, and remember you're amazing and deserve better."

Harry settled his hands and bumped their shoulders. "Thank you, Lake. You're a good friend."

Harry's tenderness made Lake choke. What a sweet, wholesome man he was. Lake was lucky to have Harry in his life, pineapple-print shirts and socks be damned. In fact, that might be something Lake could get into. The socks, anyway.

He slung an arm over Harry's shoulders and braced for Philip's approach. His ears really did stick out.

Lake could barely look at him without *remembering.* The compliments on Harry's photos, the monologues, the horrible lemon incident . . .

Philip said hello and introduced his new boyfriend, and Lake and Harry bore the moment, flushed and quiet.

Trey seemed an uptight, clever man with shocking good looks. What on Earth did he see in Philip?

Thankfully Philip and Trey quickly moved away toward the drinks station.

Harry let out a relieved breath. "What do you think of the boyfriend?"

"A little blunt. Beautiful—in a lucky-genetics-and-good-taste-in-clothes way. But he didn't seem particularly invested in Philip. I can't see it lasting."

"I hope they do," Harry said, far too kind for his own good. "I am over the whole thing. Sometimes I wonder if I was ever into him to begin with. It's not comparable, the curiosity I had with him, and what I feel—felt—with Martin . . ." He shrugged, and pulled out of the pool. "I need a drink."

Lake climbed out after him. "Make that two of us."

An hour later, he slowly sipped a martini, Knight's words

playing in his mind. *Our connection meant everything. I prefer a man who thrives in the moment. Who happily disagrees with me, who I can disagree with. A man one-hundred percent himself.*

West returned, interrupting his nerve-wrenching preoccupation.

West's somberness had vanished, and he talked and laughed loudly, but Lake noted his slight agitation. He seemed uneasy about someone seeing him flirt who shouldn't.

West shook himself. "I want to dance. Come with me?"

Lake liked the idea of dancing, but not with West. Not if it might look like something it wasn't.

Knight was laughing with his son and Amy. Lake gnawed his lip, and pointed to his drink. "Maybe later?"

West happily pivoted to Josh, standing nearby, quietly surveying the party. "Would *you* dance with me?"

Josh smiled and West tugged him toward the dance floor.

Josh excelled at dancing, of course. But this time, fiery jealousy didn't consume Lake.

Knight was alone now, hands in his pockets, staring ahead. His thoughts were elsewhere. Fairy light fell over his face, revealing a shiver of vulnerability in his expression. It made him look younger. Like he struggled with things too; wasn't quite a know-it-all.

As much as Lake didn't care how handsome Knight was, he couldn't help noticing that Knight *was.*

Tall. Strong. Confident.

He was the sexiest man Lake had ever known. *No one compared to him.*

Knight caught his eye and smiled.

Lake's heart jumped into his throat, and he smiled shakily back. He sipped his drink, feeling the prickle of Knight observing him.

He sternly told himself it might not mean anything more than friendliness.

Still, his palms grew clammy and he set his glass down before he dropped it.

Harry sidled up to Lake, slurping the last of a cocktail through a straw. "They can dance." He gestured to West and Josh. "Gathered quite the crowd."

The guests hemmed the dancefloor, watching them.

Within earshot of Lake and Harry, Philip enthusiastically exclaimed how much he liked to dance. "The Lindy Hop is my favorite. I'm wearing the right shoes for it, too."

Philip looked beseechingly at Trey, but Trey shook his head. He'd eaten too much and didn't feel like dancing.

Harry pressed his glass against Lake's chest and asked him to hold it. "Sure." Lake grabbed it. "What are you doing?"

"*I* can dance the Lindy Hop."

Lake startled. "With *Philip*?"

"It's only a dance—something I've wanted to do all evening." Harry squared his shoulders and strode over to Philip. Lake admired Harry's braveness. It was a show of forgiveness. Of moving on. Of saying they might meet each other again, so couldn't they be friendly?

"Philip," Harry said, capturing his attention. "Shall we see if they'll play *Bright Side of The Road* and show this crowd what swing dancing is?"

Slight repulsion creased Philip's mouth. He stepped back from Harry awkwardly. "I-I've eaten too much as well."

Harry dropped the hand he'd offered. "Oh. Maybe later then?"

"We're leaving soon." Philip snagged Trey by the arm, gave Harry a pathetic wave, and walked away.

Harry colored, his shoulders dropping an inch. He tried to smile. Lake moved toward him—

Knight reached him first. "I don't know the Lindy Hop, but this song should be good for a waltz, if you'd dance with me?"

Harry straightened, surprised, and nodded. Knight drew him onto the dance floor.

Lake watched, smiling, eyes watering. God. *Knight.*

The kindest, most beautiful . . . Emotion lumped in his throat, making it hard to breathe. Butterflies filled the rest of him.

Knight's gaze caught on him briefly, and Lake smiled. The purest gratitude he'd ever felt.

Knight danced better than he claimed, helped by Harry who took the lead, steering Knight's every move, eyes twinkling with humor.

They danced multiple songs, and when they were done, Josh and West both took turns dancing with Harry too.

Knight filled himself a cup of water and drank near the pool. Lake joined him; music reached them, slightly muted and more tolerable.

"Philip was thoughtless," Knight said, reading Lake's vexation at watching Philip and Trey leave through the side gate. "If I didn't already dislike him, I would now."

"How could he be so mean? To *Harry*?"

Knight sipped and stared across the pool. "He's a sweet guy. I felt tremendously for him."

"Philip should have been mean to *me*. I'm the one who messed everything up."

Knight's jaw flexed. "I'm glad he wasn't mean to you, Lake. I don't know what I would have done if he was."

Lake stuffed his hands into his pockets, pulled them out again, then fingered the cotton innards back into place. His cheeks were warm. His whole body was warm.

Cameron trudged over the grass, dragging his brother over to them.

After the obligatory catching up, Brandon looked at his Ask Austen sheet. "So, who are you two?"

Knight hesitated, and Lake held out a trembling hand. "Would you dance with me, Knightly?"

His eyebrow quirked. "Where everyone can see?"

Lake nodded, words stuck. He cleared his throat. "I've seen you dance, you're quite good, and I don't care if your son sees us."

Knight handed Cameron his cup, then stepped up to Lake. He clasped Lake's sweaty hand and drew him close. Warmth flowed over Lake from nose to tingling toe, and he gulped.

Knight poised his lips at Lake's ear. "I don't care if he sees us either."

24

Lake toed out of his shoes in the living room and flopped lengthwise onto the couch, happily exhausted. Too many feelings. Too many confessions to tell Knight. Their dance had played in Lake's mind all evening, and he couldn't stop smiling.

Knight settled into the armchair. His large hands palmed the upholstered arms and his eyes lifted slowly to Lake.

Nervousness glittered in their depths, and it was difficult to breathe. Lake shoved a hand under his chin and propped himself on his elbow. Where did he start?

He needed to know this wasn't all in his head.

"Thank you for helping me with Cameron's party. I loved how enthusiastic he got, winning the contest tied with Josh."

"Cameron's kiss sure was enthusiastic."

His wasn't the only one.

The air between them thickened with anticipation. "I had a good time, Knight." *The best.*

"Me too." Knight's mouth creased, a soft, sensuous curve to his smile.

God, would these shivers ever stop? "There was only one thing missing."

Knight raised a brow.

"A crostini station."

His look begged Lake not to joke, not now. There was more at stake. More that needed discussing. Lake nodded, swallowing, and Knight rubbed the arms of his chair. "Lake—"

The front door banged and a wash of wind swept through the house along with a grunted call for assistance.

Knight leaped to his feet, and Lake was two steps behind him. West staggered through the hall, cradling a sopping wet Harry. Pale and sporting a growing egg on his forehead, Harry's head lolled back as he giggled. "It'll be fine. I'll be fine."

West didn't look like he agreed.

"Lake, ice pack in the freezer." Knight took over and carried Harry to the couch.

Lake raced.

Lake pressed the ice pack against Harry's wound, wincing in sympathy.

"He tripped. Hit his head on the side of the pool and fell in."

West's pants were wet. Had he jumped in to save him? Good man.

Poor Harry.

"We should take him to the emergency doctor," Lake said. "He might have a concussion."

"No!" Harry exclaimed, trying to sit up. Knight steered him back down.

"He only wanted to come here," West said.

Harry groaned in pain. "That's right. No doctor. I'm sure it looks worse than it is."

For twenty minutes, Knight, West, and Lake took turns trying to convince him to go. Knight insisted he would pay if it was a matter of finance. Harry refused. "Just give me a night. If there's still pain tomorrow, I'll go."

Lake didn't love it, but he relented. "On one condition: someone stays by your side. I'll do it."

A sigh slid out of Knight. "We'll take turns."

West backed out quietly, and Lake settled in the armchair for the first shift, cocooned in Knight's lingering soapy scent.

"How did you fall?" Lake asked.

A self-deprecating laugh left Harry. "I was reading a text and tripped over a pool chair. The phone survived."

"Must've been some text."

Harry's Adam's apple bobbed up and down. "Martin. I might have asked how his date went, and he might have answered he wasn't sure there'd be another one."

Ah.

An uneasy shrug. "Never mind." He shifted the ice pack. "I think I felt something for someone else tonight."

"Felt something?"

"A spark."

Lake leaned forward, clasping his fingers. "Go on."

"I don't really want to jinx it," Harry said. "But I'm also worried because I wondered if *you* possibly liked him, and you met him first, so . . . but the way he came to my rescue! Be still my beating heart."

And what a romantic rescue it was, minus all the sogginess and pain.

"You noticed the slight flirting between us?" Lake asked.

"Slight? It was kind of obvious."

Lake hoped Knight didn't think so. "No, there is nothing there. No feelings or sparks involved."

"So you'd be . . . good? With me liking him?"

"Absolutely."

Harry sighed. "I'll never forget the feeling of his arms around me. All pain vanished, just like that. I was warm and safe and happy."

"Very romantic."

"Do you think there's any chance he might like me back?"

Lake couldn't say. More than that, he *shouldn't*. "I messed up badly with Philip, so I won't get involved with your love life again. In fact, don't tell me anything else." He didn't want to be tempted to give advice. "Just . . . read his body-language carefully. Learn from my mistake."

"Promise."

Lake nodded and winked. "I'm rooting for your happy ever after, Harry."

Much later, Knight came back downstairs. Lake tiptoed across the living room. They met under the archway and paused, Knight in his underwear and a crinkled T-shirt.

"He just fell asleep," Lake croaked. "He seems okay, but . . ."

"I'll watch out, in case."

"Thanks. Knightly?" The unspoken, taut throbbing between them needed unleashing. God, did it ever. But Harry might stir, and they were both exhausted. This wasn't the time. His lungs deflated. "Good night."

Knight inclined his head, and murmured, "Sweet dreams."

HIS DREAMS WERE SWEET INDEED.

He and Knight were tangled in bed, laughing, taking turns pinning each other down. Lake stretched over Knight, sinking into his gloriously slick, tight—

He woke up, urgently working himself to a gasping release. Spent, he soaked in the late morning funneling through the gaps between the curtains. He and Knight had to talk.

He showered and made his way downstairs, excited and anxious in a might-throw-up kind of way.

From the dining table, Knight cast him an apologetic look. Harry was smiling and coherent despite the massive bulge on his forehead; Taylor sat with Amy on his lap, kissing the freckles on her arm; Cameron was hacking at a laptop, pen behind his ear; West was helping himself to what looked like the last of the brewed coffee; Josh was sifting through must-read books Lake had stacked on the rustic buffet table.

Lake hid a sigh. He liked—even loved—this lot. But did they have to show up this morning?

He only had until four before his evening shift at the food bank.

"We've been roped into strawberry picking," Knight explained.

"Roped?" Taylor exclaimed. "You used to make me do this every year."

"Not with a crowd. And not without warning."

"More the merrier," Taylor said. "Besides, you had nothing better to do today."

Knight's grimace and fleeting glance toward Lake bubbled up hope in him. He quelled a chuckle. "Strawberries. Sounds delicious. I'm in."

"Let's carpool," Cameron said, shutting his laptop.

They split into two groups, and Lake followed Harry and Cameron to Knight's car.

Lake aimed for his usual passenger seat, but Knight insisted Harry take the front.

His head.

Right.

Cameron and Lake slid into the back, where Cameron grinned at him. "'Which of all my important nothings shall I tell you first?'"

Lake smiled weakly and—after twenty minutes of quotes—tuned him out in favor of Knight and Harry's conversation.

"Thank you for letting me stay with you," Harry was saying. "You've a beautiful house."

Lake dreamily agreed. He loved everything about the

Dixon's house too. The cozy farmhouse interior, the care that went into keeping it clean and neat, the beautiful garden filled with blossoming flowers . . . and aloe vera . . .

His gaze shot to Knight in the rearview mirror. For two beats their gazes held, until Knight returned to driving and Lake looked away, subtly adjusting himself.

At the strawberry fields, they split off into smaller groups of two and three, wandering the rows. Never far from each other.

It took an hour before Harry migrated toward Josh and West, leaving Lake and Knight alone. Not alone enough to talk. But alone enough that Lake started shivering.

Knight side-eyed Lake, popping a strawberry into his mouth. "What do you think?"

"About what?"

Knight waved across the row. "The possibility West and Josh have something going on."

"West and Josh?" Lake derided.

"You don't think so?"

"What makes *you* think so?"

"Before you joined us this morning, I caught a . . . look between them. Like an inside joke."

Lake couldn't believe it. "How many hours did you sleep last night?"

"Four, maybe."

That explained it. "You're imagining things."

Knight pivoted and looked at Lake, brown eyes steady. "I sincerely hope that's not true."

But it had to be. Surely. West and Josh? No way. "I wouldn't count on it."

West was laughing with Harry, which was far more promising. But Lake refused to share his little hope with anyone.

He meant it when he said he wouldn't get involved.

Knight's phone sounded. He passed his basket to Lake and answered. "Paul."

The wide, pleasant smile on Knight's face had Lake's stomach crunching fearfully.

"Tomorrow?" Knight murmured. ". . . Of course. . . . I'd love to meet with you in person. I'll book a flight tonight."

They shared a few more words, then Knight laughed and disengaged.

"You're flying out?" Lake asked, voice pinched.

Knight cocked his head, then gently pried Lake's rigid grip from the basket. "He has a proposal he'd like to discuss."

"A proposal?" Flashes of Paul on one knee screwed with his mind.

Knight chuckled quietly. "*Business* proposal. I'll be gone the week in Melbourne, and return Saturday morning."

"Uh-huh."

"You'll be okay in the house alone?"

Lake struggled to shake off the tightness in his gut. Knight may not have liked Josh but he *had* liked Paul and what if that reignited? What was Lake to Knight?

Why did the idea of second-best hurt so much?

"Sure," Lake mumbled. "I'll throw a kegger."

"Just clean up afterward."

What? No chastising look? "You don't care if your beautiful house is used for a kegger?"

"You have as much right to our place, and there's no one I trust more in its walls."

"You're forgetting the time I threw up in your vase!"

Knight laughed and picked more strawberries.

A melting pot of emotions, Lake drifted from row to row. When Taylor asked if he was okay, Lake nodded—the most reassurance he could cough up—and absently chatted with his best friend.

Shading his eyes with his hand, he scanned for Knight,

spotting him as he tripped and brought Harry crashing into the strawberries under him. Taylor laughed at the spectacle.

Knight quickly clambered off Harry and helped him up, apologizing.

Harry flushed and shrugged. No big deal.

Lake loved that they seemed to get along better than they had when Harry first moved in.

An hour later they set up a picnic between woods and strawberry fields. Checkered blankets were laid out, and Taylor and Amy had made dozens of sandwiches.

West sat between Lake and Harry—as far from Josh as possible, which Lake hoped Knight noticed.

"Let's play a game," Taylor said, bringing out slips of paper and pens and tape. "Who am I. Twenty questions."

They all wrote a prominent figure on the paper and the slips got redistributed and taped onto their foreheads. Ishmael. Beyoncé. Hitler. Bill Gates. Oprah. Jacinda Ardern. Elvis. And whoever Lake was.

The first rounds elicited a few laughs, but Lake was stumped. Most people had figured theirs out; he was still struggling. It didn't help that his gut churned, caught in an emotional whirlpool. He couldn't stop glancing at Knight, and thinking of Paul, and—

His turn again.

Across from him Cameron grinned. "A good one I thought up, there."

"It's your entry?" Lake said. "Then I must be Jane Austen."

Taylor ripped the slip off his forehead. "You're right, how'd you guess?"

"Of course it's his favorite author, not like he talks about anything else." Lake immediately wished he could take it back, and glanced at Cameron. "Sorry."

Cameron chuckled as if it were a joke, then grew quiet.

Redness crept up his neck and flushed his cheeks. "You're right." He nodded. "Yep."

The round continued, but the mood shifted, clouded, and Lake knew he'd gone too far.

A darting glance worsened the guilt in his gut. Knight turned away from Lake and the moment the game ended, he stood and dusted his shorts.

"I need to stretch my legs." He looked at Cameron. "Want to come with me?"

Still blushing, Cameron shoved to his feet and followed.

Guilt tightened its sick-inducing fingers around Lake. He busied himself cleaning up and carrying the blankets and empty picnic basket to Taylor's car. When he shut the trunk, he startled at Knight leaning against the side door, head bowed, intently thoughtful.

"Knight," he choked.

Knight shifted. They were alone. The others were still perusing the gift shop.

Lips set in a grim line, Knight scored a hand through his hair, frustrated. "That was unnecessarily harsh."

Regret sank Lake's insides to his knees. "Yeah, but I didn't mean to hurt him. It just came out, and he *does* talk about Austen and adapting her work a lot."

"Maybe, but he's worked hard for the privilege." Knight met his eye. "I think he only tells us because we listen and care, something his father never has."

Lake heated. He'd never wished he could take anything back so much. "I-I'm sure he'll shrug it off."

"He spent our walk asking if he was too focused on work, if he came across as boring. If everyone thought the same as you."

Lake swallowed. He'd messed up. Shown his worst side. Repulsed Knight. His eyes prickled. "I didn't mean . . ."

Knight's voice softened. "I know, Emerett."

"I'll, ah, fix it. Later." Lake couldn't bear the tangled emotions in his stomach a moment longer. Knight witnessing how unkind he could be . . . How that might affect the way he thought of Lake . . .

He averted his face and stumbled into the backseat.

Knight's figure remained pressed against the window until Taylor and Amy, exiting the gift shop, stirred him, and he trudged to his car.

Taylor said nothing about the new driving arrangements, but he slung himself in the backseat beside Lake and spent a good portion of the drive frowning curiously at him. Thankfully there was no lull to admit how confused he felt. He closed his eyes on hot tears and listened to Amy chat with West.

25

When they arrived home, Lake jumped straight into his car and headed to the food bank.

He worked alongside a smug Philip, who determined they should put the past behind them and be friends.

The last conversation Lake could handle. His mind spiraled around the picnic at the strawberry fields, and the weight of that paper against his forehead lingered. He'd been cruel, and everything Knight had said had been fair.

He needed to apologize to Cameron, soon. Urgently and completely. Needed to work on himself. Needed to be better.

The house was dark and silent when he returned, and Lake trudged to bed, hoping he'd have the chance to apologize in the morning.

But when morning came, he found Knight dragging his suitcase through the house, following the blaring hoot of a cab horn. Knight noticed him shivering in his underwear, and ignored the impatient cab driver to grab a hoodie and throw it around Lake's shoulders.

"I'm glad you're up. I was hoping to have the chance to say goodbye."

"You could have woken me."

"Yes, well. I wasn't sure about it."

Oh God, Knight hadn't forgiven him. He barely held his gaze longer than a beat.

Sorrow clogged Lake's throat; Knight rubbed his arms, let him go, and wished him a good week.

A good week would be impossible, feeling like this.

He had to fix things.

His fiery, impulsive resignation at work came unexpectedly, but as soon as he'd finished telling his boss, he felt lighter. Relieved he'd finally done it. He left early, tried and failed to get through to Knight to tell him he'd quit, and drove to his last remaining property, the bourbon distillery.

He stabbed chopsticks into takeout, gazing at the old building and the defunct Lakewood sign. It didn't feel as comforting as it had with Knight beside him.

He gave up on his noodles and rested his head against his hands on the steering wheel.

Five deep, calming breaths later, he nodded to himself and started the car.

He knew what to do.

"Who's there?" Cameron's voice was muffled.

Lake stopped rapping at the door. "You have to let me in."

"Lake?"

"You've only been good to me and I was a dick. I never should have been so thoughtless. You deserve to punch me or slap me really hard. Open the door and do that, please?"

The door *snicked* and a puzzled, puffy-eyed Cameron in flannel pajamas stood on the other side. "Will you say all that again?"

"Yes."

"Come on in."

Cameron led him to the living room, where he jumped back under a blanket on the couch. Lake hesitated and perched at the other end. His stomach grew heavy at the sight of pizza, ice cream and tissues. He'd done this to Cameron.

"It's not left my mind. It plays over and over and I can barely concentrate. I wish I could take it back. You're one of the kindest, hardest working guys I know. You've always been smart, *crazy* smart, and I've always been jealous. But jealousy is stupid and unnecessary, what I really want you to take from it is how much I admire you. How much I wish I were more like you."

"You were jealous?"

"Yes. The whole green-eyed monster thing."

"You, jealous of *me*?"

"Okay, that double-dimpled grin was the last thing I expected."'

Cameron tried and failed to control it. "Sorry, continue. You were jealous . . ."

Lake spared him a tight look that he hoped hid his bemuse-ment. "I resented how successful you are because I hate my job —which I finally quit today—and I . . ."

"Embarrassed me?"

Lake slumped. "Yeah. So I've been trying to find a way to show you how sorry I am, and I hope I found it."

Cameron's brow pinched suspiciously. "How?"

Lake Googled for pictures, and handed over his phone. Cameron stared at it, perplexed.

"Lakewood Bourbon Distillery." Lake cleared the rasp from his throat. "It's got space and is structurally in good shape. You and Brandon might have to redesign inside, but you can use it, just cover property taxes and upkeep until you're in the black. Then we can discuss rent, and I promise it'll be very reasonable."

Cameron looked at him, blinking. "I'm dreaming."

"Because I'm giving you this space to grow your channel?"

"Yes."

Lake laughed. "You're not dreaming." Long seconds passed as Cameron scrolled through pictures of the distillery. "Please say you'll take it."

Cameron let out an amazed sigh and returned his phone. "Only if you try working for Austen Studios. I've a film editing position open that I hoped you'd take."

"Wait. I was horrible to you and you're offering me a job?"

"I'm not sure honesty counts as you being horrible." Cameron picked lint off the blanket on his lap. "Besides, you're not the only one who's said I don't have a life outside of work."

Shame melted Lake. Shame, and anger at whoever else had made Cameron feel like shit. "Who—" his voice broke.

"My ex." Cameron shrugged.

"Your ex is a dick. Are we the reason for all this?" Lake motioned toward the binge foods and scrunched tissues.

"Maybe."

Lake groaned. "We *are*."

"Not just you and the ex. Some of this is because of . . ." Cameron screwed his eyes shut and his throat bulged. "Josh."

Josh? "What did Josh say?"

"Less what he said than what he did."

"What did he do?"

Cameron sniffed and opened his eyes. "He fell in love with West."

Lake laughed—surely Cameron was having him on. "I'm not following."

Had Knight read them correctly all along?

Was Knight *ever* wrong?

"I liked Josh. A stupid crush that would never have worked anyway."

The anguish in Cameron's voice made Lake's belly lurch.

God, wanting someone so bad and realizing they didn't want you back . . .

Would this be him when Knight got back? When they talked? Would Lake feel that desperate pain of unrequited adoration?

Sympathy for Cameron wrenched through him. "I'm sorry." He frowned. "Josh and West?"

"Josh told me last night. They've been together for years. Remember how I hooked Josh up with West's number for his time in England? He used it, and they hit it off."

"Why the secrecy?"

"West didn't want anyone to know until after he'd told his parents, which he's been doing over the last couple of weeks. It's why he missed Taylor's party, and why he's been staying at Taylor's. It hasn't been going well. He's being cut off from his parents and shunned by his community. West picked up the last of his things after our strawberry outing, and went straight to Josh."

"Josh came over and told you immediately?"

"Probably only because I saw their . . . very affectionate embrace while parking my car." Cameron grabbed a tissue and blew his nose. "It's officially no longer a secret, and I'm happy Josh is happy. I'm just . . ."

Lake sidled over the couch and locked an arm around Cameron. "Yeah." He shook his head. "I can't believe . . . West and Josh. This whole time—West bought the wedding cake."

Cameron nodded.

Lake ran over the weekend in his mind again. Everything West had said, done . . . His sudden vanity outside Josh's house; that "much nicer here" when he'd sat next to Lake within perfect view of Josh at the window; outside the bakery—West had meant to meet Josh for a sneaky rendezvous. His idea the winners of the Ask Austen game should dance, kiss—he wanted an excuse to break free from the secrecy. That call with his parents at the party—

"Poor West. And Josh. Having to hide like that. Poor you." And Harry. Poor him, too. He'd been all dreamy-eyed since West's gallant rescue. "I'll need a moment to process it."

"Or a few," Cameron agreed.

LAKE SHOULD PROBABLY TELL HARRY THAT WEST WAS OFF THE market.

But.

Harry had a big audition on Friday, and Lake shouldn't distract him from learning his lines. Besides, the likelihood he bumped into West before Friday evening was low.

Lake waited until after his audition.

Harry slouched into the living room and flopped onto Knight's usual armchair. "I didn't get it."

Lake winced. "I don't know if this is helpful, but Cameron told me he and his brother are holding auditions for a costume drama next week. He wanted to send you a script."

Harry scrambled upright. "Are you kidding me?"

"Bad timing?"

"The *best*. I needed to get my mind off today's near miss. Costume drama." Harry lounged back into the armchair dreamily, lips lifting softly. "I'll nail this."

Lake smirked. "Have fun doing that." His smile waned and he rubbed his thighs. Time to break the news—

"By the way." Harry looked over at Lake. "I banged into West after my audition."

"Oh, you did?" Definitely time to gently let Harry's hopes down. "About West—"

"He was hand in hand with Josh."

Lake blinked in confusion, face pinching. What?

Harry continued, "Can you believe it?"

What Lake couldn't believe was how easy-going and jovial Harry was about it.

Not even a flicker of disappointment.

Harry sat forward, voice serious. "You look shocked. Are you sad? Did you like him?"

Like him? No! Shocked? Well, a bit. He'd expected to drag Harry to the grocery store for ice cream. "I'm beginning to see how bad I am at reading people. I thought you'd be bummed West was taken."

"Me? Why?" Harry cocked his head, frowning. "Did you think I was interested in him?"

"I mean, it's good you're not? I was waiting all week to tell you because I didn't want it to affect your audition."

"So you knew."

"Yes." Lake's frown deepened. "You said you had a spark. You've been ultra-happy all week, watching all those rom-coms. Singing dreamily as you tended the garden."

"I was never into West. I barely know him."

Fear wormed inside him, and he rubbed his palms against his thighs harder. "But—"

Harry chuckled. "You misunderstood me."

Lake's voice thickened; fear multiplied. "What do you mean?"

Another laugh. "I didn't want to jinx it, but I assumed you knew who I meant. Especially since you've been flirting with him."

Terror had Lake frozen on the couch. "Are you talking about Knightly?"

Harry nodded. "Thought it was obvious."

"But you said he came to your rescue. I thought you meant falling into the pool!"

"That was good of West, but I meant the other Knight in shining armor." He giggled at his pun. "I was embarrassed when Philip turned me down for the Lindy Hop, and then Knight swooped in and took the hurt away. I felt cared for. Seen, liked. He's such a good, kind man, reminds me so much of Mar—anyway, does this change things?"

Lake paced the length of the hearth. How could he have misunderstood Harry? Why had he assumed and not clarified? Had he not learned anything since Philip?

His stomach lodged itself somewhere around his knees.

"It does change things then." Harry's disappointment was palpable, and Lake couldn't look at him.

Knight had warned Lake about messing in others' love lives, and look at the mess he'd made with Harry. Look how much Lake had screwed with him. Angling him away from Martin, foisting him toward Philip who didn't care for him at all, convincing him Lake didn't have feelings for West when Harry had meant Knight . . .

Knight, who Lake . . .

But did Knight feel the same way? Lake thought he'd felt understanding pass between them at the Ask Austen party. Or was that also misunderstood? What if these momentous feelings were only on his side?

He'd read Philip wrong. Harry, too. Who wasn't to say he'd dreamed up *this* wondrous connection too?

Lake spun on his heel, facing Harry. "You spent Sunday evening with Knight while I worked. Did you have more sparks? Did they feel reciprocated?"

Harry bowed his head, biting his lip. "Maybe?"

The word hit him like a punch. Lake collapsed onto the couch and stared at the fireplace. Pain ripped through him like a burning arrow.

His throat closed, his jaw clenched, his hands balled the edge of the cushion. He didn't want Knight loving anyone but him. Not Paul, not Josh, not Harry. He wanted Knight's sole loving attention, and he wanted it . . . forever.

God, Lake had been so blind. Clueless of his own feelings. If he were honest, if he really dwelled in his history with Knight . . . he'd felt this way for a while. A seed when they first met, slowly growing, until these last weeks . . . the springtime of its life, blooming for the first time. The most beautiful flower Lake had ever known.

Beautiful, and delicate. Standing tall in a field of grass, wind pummeling it from every direction. Would it last? Would Knight tend to him with as much care as he did everything else in his garden, and in life?

Or was it doomed to shrivel and die?

Lake's insides knotted as he glanced at Harry. *Maybe.* What had he meant?

Knight had danced with him, then cradled him in his arms when West had brought him home. He had offered him the front seat to the strawberry fields, and weeks ago, had stopped Lake from burning his shirts—even telling Lake that he liked Harry just as he was.

Oh, God.

"When did you have another 'spark'?" Lake did not sound like himself.

Harry hesitated. "At the strawberry fields. He toppled over me. I thought he did it on purpose. And . . ."

There was *more?*

"He asked me if I was still in contact with Martin." Lake frowned, and Harry continued, "It felt like he was fishing. To see how available I am?"

"What did you say? What did he say?"

"We didn't get to finish our conversation. But I was hoping to do so this weekend."

Fear was a physical ache in him now. "What if it was just small talk? What if falling over you was an accident?"

"I was paying close attention, like you told me to. He definitely colored after the fall, and he was so kind on Sunday night. He made us dinner, even though you weren't there. Pasta with a paired white wine."

Lake rose once more to shaky feet. He was about to throw up. "I . . . I . . . This can't be happening. Knight is . . ." His voice cracked, and he turned away and strode out of the room. *He's mine.*

26

K night wasn't his though. Lake just wanted him to be.
He climbed into Knight's bed like he'd sneakily been doing all week. Sheets cocooned him as he breathed in Knight's scent on his pillow. He read the chat messages from the week. All very Knightly messages, wishing him a good day and good night. Nothing that suggested more. Or . . . less.

Only one stuck out. From the group chat, where Taylor had unjustly gushed about Lake's generosity in letting Cameron use his distillery.

Knight: Is that so?

Taylor: Lake's the best.

Knight: 🤍

What did that mean? How could it make him hope this violently? He groaned into the pillow, thrashing his fist against the mattress.

He'd been foolish. He'd made a mess of everyone's love lives, including his own. If he hadn't meddled to begin with, Harry wouldn't have lived with them, and any feelings between Knight and him wouldn't exist.

Did feelings exist?

Could Harry have misread Knight?

He had to know.

Lake: I know you care about me.

Lake: But I need to know . . .

Do I come first?

Lake stopped himself from typing more, then deleted the messages.

He set his phone facedown atop Moby Dick, and sighed. He hadn't read a single page since Knight left. How could he hope he was someone special, when he never finished anything? When he'd shown Knight how horrible he could be?

How could he hope so strongly when he hadn't done anything to deserve Knight?

He sat up and grabbed the book. A fifth left. He could do this.

Lake cracked it open, removed the tabloid bookmark, and read.

LAKE GULPED AND SET THE BOOK DOWN. HIS PHONE TOLD HIM it was six in the morning. He'd read through the night.

He should be exhausted, not bubbling with eagerness to tell Knight. Just because he'd read to The End, didn't mean Knight would care. Lake rolled out of bed, making a mental note to make it properly before Knight returned, slipped on some jeans and a T-shirt, and snuck downstairs. Sleep was beyond him.

He tiptoed down the hall, not wanting to wake Harry—

His bedroom door was open?

The bed was untouched and there was none of Harry's usual mess. No sign of anything Harry.

"Harry?" he called, like the man might emerge spontaneously, at six in the morning.

Lake retreated to the living room, and into the kitchen—

A note.

Harry thought it was better if he didn't stay there.

Lake slumped into the garden. Garfield found him on the cold gazebo bench, and Lake cuddled her close. An ache washed over him and the hairs on his arms rose.

How could the brink of happiness be so torturous?

He *loved*—

"Knight!" Lake stood abruptly, Garfield coming with him. "What are you doing here?" His voice shook, bewildered, apprehensive, hopeful.

Knight looked taller in the morning glow. Hair darker, chin squarer. No trace of laughter creased his mouth or his eyes. He'd not shaved this morning, nor perhaps combed his hair, and it added to the urgency emanating from him.

He jaunted up the gazebo steps and strode forward, halting abruptly before him. Soulful brown eyes connected with his, and Garfield meowled at how hard Lake was clutching her.

He loosened his hold, and she jumped out of his arms. Lake felt exposed without her. He hugged himself, catching sight of Knight's dusty dress shoes. "Did you walk from the airport?"

"Not exactly." Knight's voice sounded raw. "I saw your messages before you deleted them. They popped up on my screen, and I grabbed my things and caught the earliest plane back I could. Too early to wake you like I wanted. So I left the taxi a few blocks back and took my time walking."

Lake's mouth dried. "Not too early. I-I couldn't sleep."

"That makes two of us." Knight ran a hand through his hair. "Can I sit with you?"

They sat. Lake's chest seized with a million butterflies. "Emerett . . ." Knight stood again.

Lake had never seen him so flustered. There was nothing happy about his expression; he seemed tense. Worried, determined. What did that mean? "Should we walk? Around the garden?"

"It does need a water."

Silently, they set up the hose and Lake took charge of the nozzle, aiming it at the base of the honeysuckle. Knight kept looking at him; he felt the prickle on his profile.

If he would smile, Lake would know this imminent conversation would be the one he'd hoped for. But Knight had likely come home early to apologize for crossing lines with him, for confusing his feelings. He was sensible and caring, and he wanted to clarify their friendship face to face.

Lake had to say something. Break the tension crackling with nervous energy between them. "You were right, by the way."

"Right?" Knight asked.

"About Josh and West having a thing."

"Yes. Were you disappointed? You seemed to really get along with West."

Lake turned to him, water pulsing to their side. "I'm not into West, Knight. Not that way. At all."

Knight's stiff posture eased. He reached for the hose, and their warm fingers brushed as he took it over. "I hoped . . . I'm relieved to hear it."

That quiet, shaky exhale.

Lake's chest fluttered.

Knight steered the hose toward the flowerbed closer to him. "Every mention of his name turned me into someone I didn't like."

Lake's gaze shot to Knight's profile. "On paper, he seemed like a good match, but . . . He is not for me."

"I was envious."

Lake's words tangled in his throat. "Like I was with Josh? Am currently, with Harry?"

A darted, confused glance. "Harry?"

"Aren't there sparks between you? You made him dinner with paired wine. You fell on him at the strawberry fields."

"I've been cooking dinner for you both for weeks, and I fell by accident!"

"So, you weren't fishing about Martin to see if Harry was available?"

"Good Lord." Knight faced him. "I did not race home to speak to Harry. Was that what you needed to know? When I read that message I thought—"

"That's not what that message was about." Lake looked away, and Knight returned his focus to the drenched flowerbed.

"What do you need to know?" Softly.

Lake understood. "I'm . . . I'm not sure I need you to tell me anymore." He felt the truth like he'd never felt anything in his life. It lifted him so high, he was soaring.

"You don't?" Knight's Adam's apple jutted.

Lake touched Knight's arm, skated his fingers over Knight's whitened knuckles and twisted the nozzle to Off. "I don't."

Knight whisked around. "I have to tell you. I've held back so long, waiting for you to see how much I care, and your messages . . ." He looked Lake desperately in the eye.

Oh God, he'd misunderstood. Lake didn't need to know because now it was finally clear to him how Knight felt, not because he didn't *want* to know—

He tried to interject, but Knight was . . . impassioned. "I

do care about you, Emerett. I care about you so goddamn much. Not just as a friend."

Lake stepped close to Knight's resolute stance. He pressed a palm to Knight's chest and spread his fingers over the soft fabric of his T-shirt. His voice trembled. "No, not as a friend." He looked up, flushing. "I think you . . . love me?"

Knight sucked in a deep breath. Swallowed. Whispered, "So very much."

"How long?"

"A while. Before I picked you up from the police station last year. I didn't think you felt the same. Until . . . everything since the wedding made me wonder. Made me . . . hope. The things you did and said, I . . . But even as I grew surer, I knew you were oblivious to it."

Lake folded into Knight, resting his forehead against his shoulder, groaning. "I've been so blind. With everything. Harry, Philip, West." His nose brushed Knight's neck, and he breathed in the scent of spring. "Most of all you."

"Reading you has been a pastime for months, but right now I need spoilers. Do you feel the same?"

Lake murmured, echoing Knight. "I'm not feeling your heartbeat for theatrics."

Knight cupped Lake's face. His serious eyes searched Lake's. "I don't expect undying commitment, but I need to know—"

Lake surged forward and kissed him. The lightest press of their lips, one beat, two, three.

Knight gasped, hands slipping to his waist, his nape, squeezing as he deepened their kiss. They held each other, both trembling, each holding the other up. "I can't believe it."

"Neither can I," Lake admitted. "I was scared you saw me differently after how horrible I was to Cameron."

Knight kissed him again, sincere, tender. "You made a mistake. You also apologized—and your distillery? What a wonderful way to help Cameron. You're a kind, generous, loving man."

Lake grinned. He did like all this praise . . . "Anything else?"

Knight laughed. "I love how much you live in the moment, how you inspire so many people, how you always find a way to make me laugh. You make our house a home."

Lake's heart tripped. "Our?"

"Yes, Emerett. Our."

"Oh my God. I just got it."

Knight raised a brow.

"*I'm* why you're single."

"No one else could hold a candle to you."

Lake startled, more realizations slamming into him. "You never were into Paul."

"No. You certainly ran off with that theory."

"Our first kiss . . . you weren't just proving a point. You wanted it."

"And a million more, if you'll give them to me."

Lake began pacing, cringing at all the signs he should have seen. "That fancy dinner . . . Was that a date?"

"I'd hoped so."

"I brought Harry along!"

"It certainly cemented my understanding of your cluelessness."

"Karaoke." Lake halted before Knight. "You're The One That I Want. Holy shit, slay me already."

Joyous laughter.

Lake glared. "Is there any other sign I missed?"

"Other than watering you during your Philip-Shakespeare palaver, and letting you sleep in my bed, and making love to you, I think you have it."

Lake collapsed against Knight's chest and buried a mortified whimper in his shirt.

Knight encircled him in tight, comforting arms, and kissed the top of his head. "I like that I can do this now." He kissed him again. "I like it very much."

"I like it too." Lake pulled back, and that unfamiliar shyness took him hostage once more. "Could we go to bed?"

27

Lake padded inside Knight's bedroom and quietly shut the door.

Dawn hedged the drawn curtains, giving everything a silvery glow. Standing in the middle of the medallion-print rug, Knight took in the state of his room, including yesterday's clothes that Lake folded over the trunk at the end of the bed, and the twisted sheets.

Lake hugged himself. "I, um . . . I . . ."

Knight faced him, tenderness filling his gaze. He drew Lake close. "How long?"

"All week." Lake flushed, dropping his arms. "I missed you."

Knight's kiss bloomed through Lake.

He pulled back, breathing in deeply, and searched Knight's eyes. Glistening, touched, happy.

Shivers zinged between them, and Lake questioningly clutched the hem of Knight's shirt.

Knight raised his arms.

They undressed one another, trading keepsake smiles. Soft, tender, adoring.

Calloused fingers glided down Lake's sides to the small of his back, and their naked, aching bodies meshed.

Giddiness rose through him from heel to scalp and his heart pounded. They fell onto the bed in a rush of gravity, parting briefly with laughter.

A mad craving for closeness overwhelmed him.

Lake rolled atop of Knight and stretched his arms above

his head, clasping his wrists against the mattress. Lake smiled down at him and dipped for a kiss. Their noses grazed and their lips connected on a wondrous sigh.

How could Lake have not seen Knight's glorious feelings for him? How could he have been so blind to his own?

He'd make up for lost time. For every evening Knight had gone to bed nursing an ache in his large, kind, beautiful heart.

Lake molded himself to Knight. Soft kisses became passionate, deep, searing.

Still, neither spoke.

Lake found the condoms, the lube. Knight steered Lake's slippery fingers, a whisper tickling Lake's neck below the ear. "Take me?"

Chest and cock throbbed. Lake shimmied down, trembling, and gripped Knight's base. He lowered his head. He'd dreamed of tasting Knight, of taking him deep into his mouth, of giving him so much pleasure he couldn't *think*.

He flicked his tongue over salty pre-come, lubed fingers playing at Knight's entrance, dipping into the soft ring.

A deep moan vibrated through Lake, so open, so trusting, so real. Lake wanted to undo him. He sucked Knight into his mouth, tongue sliding up and down his shaft in humming strokes. In tandem, Lake worked lube into him, slowly, teasing him open.

Knight bucked with taut, needy grunts.

Opening his throat wide, Lake took his pulsing cock deep as he stretched three fingers into him.

Knight cried out, gently gripped his hair, and steered him off. He grabbed the condom and shakily ripped into it.

Lake buckled against Knight's broad shoulders in a plea-sured gasp as Knight swiftly rolled the latex over him.

They crashed into a desperate kiss, falling back to the mattress. Lake hooked Knight's leg, and their eyes met. The world spun and untangled, everything clear. Everything *right*.

He nudged Knight's entrance, and Knight nodded, threading a sure hand through Lake's hair, kissing him again. Lake breached him, gasping at the tight, slippery heat. He held himself still, aching. "Are you—?"

Knight cupped a cheek, thumb rubbing over the bow of his lip. "Perfect. Keep going."

Lake eased in, Knight throbbing around him. Oh God, too good. He melted into mindless babbling. *I won't last. Good thing we can do this again and again. The rest of our lives.*

Knight entwined their fingers and squeezed.

Butterflies invaded Lake's chest, and he slanted a fervent kiss against Knight's slackened lips. He rotated his hips and pulled out to the tip.

Knight arched up as Lake pushed in again, a gravelly uttered "Emerett" stealing Lake's breath.

Another kiss. This one emblazoned with desire, the headiness of emotion giving way to baser instincts.

Lake pushed into him, eagerly, burrowing as deep as he could.

Knight wrapped his legs around Lake, urging him for more, meeting every thrust. Every move stoked their pleasure until Lake didn't know where he ended and Knight started. They were a cocoon of grunts, gasps, shudders, pleas. The bed shook, and they breathed in each other's mindless whispers.

Kisses tickled Lake's neck, wet heat puffed against his ear. Lake bucked into the perfect glove of slick friction. Relentlessly plunged into Knight, angling where it made him thrash the most.

Their skin grew damp; their gazes held hungrily, like they wanted to be connected forever. Ecstasy hammered through him, hot in his cock and his chest, and he felt Knight's pleasure crescendo in time.

He dropped kiss after kiss, wherever his lips landed. He

sucked in that wonderful earthy scent. Each shared breath fueled his pleasure. He couldn't get enough.

"God, Knightly."

Their gazes hooked, and startling tenderness slammed into Lake, propelling him to a shuddering orgasm. Wave after wave of perfect release spilled into Knight, and Knight tightened around him, stiffening in pleasure, a groan of satisfaction against Lake's ear as he came between their stomachs.

Lake collapsed over Knight, limp. His cock slipped free, and he lazily drew off the condom, tying and tossing it off the bed. He used the nearest T-shirt to wipe Knight dry, hushing his reprimanding look. Knight gave in with a soft laugh and sagged back against the pillows.

Head resting on Knight's shoulder, Lake savored the feel of Knight gathering him close and catching a contented breath.

A feathered kiss touched Lake's forehead. Embraced in each other's arms, they fell asleep.

When Lake woke, sunlight beamed at the edges of the curtains, and Knight, awake and reading, was haloed in gold.

Once more, Lake had drooled over his stomach, and once more, with a glance under *Moby Dick*, Knight thought nothing of it.

"There's no bookmark in here."

Lake snuck up under Knight's arm, curling into him. He glanced at the opened book. "Don't need it anymore, I finished it last night."

Knight hummed. "In that case, I believe I owe you some praise."

Lake grinned. "Gimmie. Put the book down." He lightly bit Knight's shoulder. "There's only one Dick I want you holding right now."

A snorted laugh. Brown eyes blazed, and the book hit the floor . . .

After, Lake tucked himself against Knight's side. His arm

was wrapped around Knight's belly, and he felt him catching his breath.

Dizzying lightness surged inside Lake, filling him up. Everything had snicked into place, like he and Knight were lock and key.

"What are you thinking?" Knight murmured.

"I'm so happy." The moment after he said it, guilt punched into him and he lurched upright. "No, I'm not." At Knight's confusion, Lake exclaimed, "Harry!"

HOW HAD HE FORGOTTEN?

Lake showered frantically. He needed to find Harry and apologize.

Knight palmed steadying hands on his soap-slippery shoulders and held his gaze through the spray of water.

"He's probably at his grandma's. He'll be okay."

"Physically, sure. But what about his feelings? You were right all along, Knightly. I should have been more careful. I have to fix this." Lake grimaced. "Will you help me?"

An hour and a few text messages from Knight to Harry later, Knight cast Lake a grim smile over the dining table.

Lake gulped the last of his coffee. "What's the matter? Is he okay?"

"Harry's fine. But you've always been sensitive about this, and I'm not sure how you'll take it."

Lake's mind was spiraling. "Take what?"

"He's staying with Martin."

Lake blinked.

Knight reached over and caressed the back of his hand. "I know you don't like them caring for each other, Emerett. But I wish you didn't see it as forbidden."

Lake shook his head. "I did find it weird in the beginning, but . . ." He looked into Knight's eyes. "Love knows no boundaries." He flipped his hand around, two fingers pressing against Knight's erratic pulse. "Would you come with me to talk to them?"

Knight did, and Martin welcomed them into his apartment with a hearty smile. He showed them to Harry, who lay with a blanket up to his chin on the couch.

"Should I, er, leave you?" Martin offered.

Lake shook his head. "What I have to say is for both of you."

That remark had Harry sitting up, frowning.

Lake felt Knight's warmth behind him, and swallowed.

He pulled torn bits of paper out of his pocket and pieced them together on the glass coffee table. "I pulled these out of the fireplace, Harry."

Harry's eyes watered as he read the words on the page.

"You said you were purging yourself of unrequited feelings," Lake said. "For ages I thought you were referring to Philip. But, you never really cared for Philip, did you?"

Harry shook his head. "I wanted to, but—" He glanced at Martin, flushing.

Martin made a small noise at the back of his throat, and Harry tossed the blankets off his lap and stood. Shyly, he held out his hand to Martin, and Martin's step stuttered as he grasped it.

Harry drew him to the coffee table. "Every page in my diary was about you." He glanced guiltily at Lake, but raised his chin defiantly. "I'm sorry, Lake. But—"

"The only sorry should be from me, Harry," Lake said. "I never should have steered you away from Martin. What you have is yours, and no one's opinion should take that away."

Martin sank to his knees and read the page over again. He looked up at Harry, eyes glistening, and Harry knelt, rubbing Martin's arms, asking if he was okay—

Martin kissed him.

GOD, LAKE LOVED LOVE.

Harry boldly told Lake he wasn't returning with him. He had a place at Martin's. And Lake backed triumphantly into Knight, curling Knight's arms around his waist, effectively giving their relationship status away.

Harry smiled and told them to hurry off, he had important things to . . . do.

The car ride home was spent deciding what Lake would wear to Harry's wedding. They parked outside of their home, and Knight told him to go ahead while he helped Cameron, who was struggling to lift a massive armchair out of a trailer.

Lake sprang up the Dixon—Dixon-Lakewood?—porch and halted, tip of the key in the door.

What *was* that?

The groaning of floorboards. He heard it again.

Fear jumped into Lake's throat. Knight was helping Cameron. Harry was with Martin.

He stole around the side of the house. Through the window, he caught a shadowy figure.

Intruder.

Lake grabbed a baseball bat from the back shed and let himself in through the back door. His grip was sweaty as he snuck through the hall and followed the sound of the TV to the living room doorway. He jumped into the room with a warrior-cry, brandishing the bat—

Taylor leaped in fright onto the couch, hands raised.

"Taylor?"

"Lake?"

Lake dropped his arm.

"What the hell are you doing scaring me with my own bat?" Taylor slowly uncurled from fright and slumped back into the couch cushions.

Lake cringe-smiled and tossed himself into Knight's armchair. The end of the bat smacked against the floor. "You scared the shit out of me."

Taylor rolled his eyes. He looked nothing like his dad. Only echoes of Knight came through in some of his expressions. Especially the leveled looks. Like the one Taylor was giving him now.

"What the hell are you doing here?" Lake said.

Taylor found the remote and switched off the TV. He rubbed his thighs and looked at Lake. "Actually, I came to chat with you."

"What's so urgent you had to break into the house?"

"I used the spare key. Is it really breaking in if I grew up here?"

"Yeah, maybe not. A heads up next time though. You wouldn't want to give your old man a heart-attack."

Taylor laughed, nervously. "I'm more worried about giving myself a heart attack."

Lake frowned, throat constricting. "What do you mean?"

"I'm not blind, Lake. I got the Josh-part wrong, but I didn't misread Dad's mood. He's in love, and I think," Taylor met his gaze, "he's in love with you."

Lake's breath hitched. His grip tightened on Taylor's bat.

Taylor continued, "Everything you said at the Ask Austen party. You meant it, didn't you?"

Lake unfroze. He stood and dropped the bat into the chair, giving up on explaining the backstory. He met Taylor's eyes. "I meant every word of it. I love your dad."

Taylor's gaze shot sideways. Knight stood in the doorway, clutching his keys.

The air thickened, weighted with honeysuckle and Lake's admission.

Dropping his keys, Knight strode toward him, cradled his head, and kissed him. The power of that simple kiss stunned Lake. So brief, yet packed with an intensity Lake had never felt before. An exclamation mark. A *yes* to anything Lake could ever ask for.

Knight rested his forehead against Lake's, mirroring the smile pulling at his lips. "Any questions, Taylor?" His voice was steady, confident, sure.

Taylor picked Garfield up and planted her on his lap. "Only about a hundred, Dad. But"—he smooched Garfield between the ears—"for now . . . I'm happy for you guys."

Knight smiled widely, and Lake let out a shuddering breath of relief.

"Anything else pressing?" Knight asked Taylor.

"Do I have to call him dad, too?"

Lake stifled a laugh against Knight's shoulder, "Say yes."

Knight cherishingly petted his hair. "No. Now if that's all, you have a choice. Kindly head home, or brace for a heart attack."

Garfield scurried free as Taylor leaped to his feet. He

paused in his haste, just long enough to grin back at them, then kicked off out of sight with a laugh.

The front door shut, and Knight linked their fingers. "First lunch."

Lake squeezed his hand, pulling him back around. "First, one other thing." He slid his arms around Knight's neck and kissed those ever-smiling lips. "I love you."

THE END

About the author

A bit about me: I'm a big, BIG fan of slow-burn romances. I love to read and write stories with characters who slowly fall in love.

Some of my favorite tropes to read and write are: Enemies to Lovers, Friends to Lovers, Clueless Guys, Bisexual, Pansexual, Demisexual, Oblivious MCs, Everyone (Else) Can See It, Slow Burn, Love Has No Boundaries.

I write a variety of stories, Contemporary MM Romances with a good dollop of angst, Contemporary lighthearted MM Romances, and even a splash of fantasy.
My books have been translated into German, Italian, French, Spanish, and Thai.

Contact: http://www.anytasunday.com/about-anyta/
Sign up for Anyta's newsletter and receive a free e-book:
http://www.anytasunday.com/newsletter-free-e-book/

About the illustrator

Lauren Dombrowski is a comic artist and illustrator based in the Chicago area. Their previous artistic publication contributions include internal illustration work to *Conventionally Yours* (2020) by Annabeth Albert and *Say You'll Be Nine* (2020) by Lucy Lennox. They have also contributed comic work and illustrations to *Dates! Volume 3* (2019) and *A Survey of Queer Looks 1890—2018* (2018) with Margins Publishing, as well as *Tabula Idem: A Queer Tarot Comic Anthology* (2017) with Fortuna Media.

Website: laurendombrowski.com
Twitter: @callmekitto
Instagram: @l.e.d.light
E-mail: ldombrowskiart@gmail.com

Printed in Great Britain
by Amazon

61424815R00147